MAMALI

A STORY OF MANY

KALYANI MOHANTY

Index

Acknowledgements

I extend my heartfelt thanks to everyone who helped bring this book to life. Any mistakes are entirely my responsibility.

I am deeply grateful to Dr. Sandeep Mohanty for his inspiring discussions and to Mrs. Puspanjali Mohanty for her unwavering support. A sincere thank you to my parents, friends, and family members. I also appreciate Professor Sumantra Bhattacharya, who has always believed in me. Special thanks to my publishing team for making this book a reality.

Dedication

This book is dedicated to my cherished support system—my family and friends—whose steadfast encouragement has propelled me forward. Your unwavering belief in me has been the driving force behind this journey, and I am profoundly thankful for the love and inspiration you've provided.

In loving memory of Mr. Krutibas Mohanty, whose enduring spirit continues to guide and inspire me. Though deeply missed, your influence on my life remains timeless.

A sincere thank you to Professor Sumantra Bhattacharya for their invaluable wisdom and guidance, shaping my perspective and serving as a constant wellspring of motivation.

This dedication is extended to all the dreamers, believers, and seekers of inspiration. May this book resonate with your spirit and ignite the spark of possibility within.

I express my deepest gratitude to each one of you for being an integral part of this literary journey.

Preface

Before you dive into this book, let me introduce you to the story inside. This is a story about a girl who faces many challenges and must decide whether to give up or keep pushing forward.

As you read, imagine yourself right there with her during the tough times, cheering her on during the good moments. This story isn't just any story; it's an invitation to be part of her journey and feel the struggles she encounters.

Life gets really hard for her, and she has to decide whether to stop or keep going. You'll see tough parts that make her think about quitting and moments that push her to keep trying. This story invites you to be with her as she deals with challenges and makes choices.

Every word is a glimpse into her journey, where deciding whether to give up or keep going becomes a really big deal. So, let's start this adventure, and I hope the pages ahead let you feel her struggles and root for her choices.

Chapter 1:
The Devastating News

It had been ages since I'd seen anyone I knew or received any calls. It had been a rough week with exams. Then, on a Sunday morning around 10:00 a.m. in 2011, there was a knock at my door. "Who's there?" I asked, curious. "It's me, the Hostel Warden," the reply came. "There's a landline call for you, Mamali!"

In moments, Mamali found herself running through the silent halls, Mamali felt a flutter of excitement. The strict rules of no phones in the hostel made this call a rare bridge to her past life.

Picking up the phone, my heart leaped at my grandfather's voice. "Mamali, my dear, how are you?" he asked with warmth.

"I've missed you, Grandpa," she replied with a smile in her voice despite the miles between them.

"When will you come to visit me?" I couldn't help but ask.

"Soon, my lady," he promised. "I've missed you too. Listen, I have a special gift for you for your 21st birthday. But, you'll get it only if you come to see me. Will you?"

"I'll try my best, Grandpa. I can't wait." I said.

Hearing my low tone, he asked, "What's wrong, my dear?"

"It's these exams, Grandpa," I confessed, my voice a mix of frustration and tiredness. "They're all I can think about, and I'm scared I won't do well."

He told me, "What matters is how we deal with hard times. You're ready for this. You're prepared, and you're capable. Remember, the effort you put in now is the foundation for your success. Believe in yourself."

To My Safe Space

After a year's wait, the day to see Mr. Perfect finally arrived. The journey, though six hours long, felt like a moment with my heart racing with excitement. The time apart had felt like an eternity, magnified beyond the 365 days that had passed.

As I stepped off the bus, there he was—Mr. Perfect—waiting to welcome me with open arms. Our reunion was emotional, a mix of tears and smiles, as if no time had passed between us. "Hey, Mr. Perfect, acting like a child, aren't we?" I teased him gently, wrapped securely in his embrace. "Smile, please. I'm here, safe and sound."

His voice trembled with emotion. "I feared I might not see you again before my last breath."

"How could that be? Let's not dwell on tears. I promise to visit every month," I assured him, wiping away my tears.

"Is that a promise?" he asked, hoping to light up his face.

"A pinky promise," I confirmed, our fingers locking in a vow.

During those 32 hours with Mr. Perfect, every second was golden. We got lost in card games, not really caring who won or lost, but just enjoying the jokes and stories that flowed. We spent time in the garden, our hands in the soil, feeling connected to the earth and to each other. Fishing was a whole new level of fun, waiting quietly together until we caught something for lunch.

The highlight was the meal Mr. Perfect prepared—Patrapoda Macha. This dish, fish wrapped and cooked in banana leaves, a delicacy from our part of eastern India, was more than just food. It was a taste of home, of tradition, and of Mr. Perfect's love. Each bite was a burst of flavours, the fish tender and infused with aromatic spices and smokiness from the banana leaves. It was a meal that lingered on my palate and in my heart, a memory to cherish.

As the hours slipped away, filled with laughter and shared stories, I knew it was time to leave. Saying goodbye felt like I was leaving part of myself behind. Walking to the bus station, I felt a mix of sadness and the pressure of upcoming exams. Those precious moments with Mr. Perfect were a break from everything waiting for me back at the hostel. But as I headed back to my studies, the memories of our time together kept me going, reminding me of the love and happiness that's always there, waiting for me beyond my textbooks.

After my finals, I checked my phone and saw 32 missed calls from an unknown number. I felt worried. Something wasn't right. When I tried to call back, no one answered. It was just silent, which made me even more anxious.

Then I got the news: Mr. Perfect, my grandfather, was very sick. This news made me feel really sad. I couldn't believe it. My world, always brighter with him around, suddenly felt empty.

I rushed home immediately, driving 300 kilometers that seemed to take forever. Each mile made me more anxious about what was waiting for me.

When I arrived, the house was too quiet. It was hard walking into our home knowing Mr. Perfect was fighting for his life in the hospital.

Mr. Perfect was not just my grandfather. He was my closest friend and the person who taught me about life. He showed me how to be kind, how to trust, and how to support others. He shaped who I am.

Sitting in the quiet of our home, I thought about all his lessons and our memories together. These thoughts helped me feel a little better. He taught me so much about caring for others and being a good person.

Even though he was very ill, his influence on me was strong. His wisdom and love were like a light in the darkness, guiding me on how to live better.

Returning home from the hospital knowing he was getting better brought relief. We had all been worried, but now we felt thankful he was recovering.

The next days were hard but also brought clarity. Mr. Perfect's lessons about love and life stayed with me. He taught that love is about actions and making positive changes.

His words helped me see challenges as opportunities to grow. He believed in being kind and living a meaningful life. These ideas have changed how I view relationships and challenges.

Standing in our house, surrounded by his presence, I knew I had to live by his teachings. His saying, "Nothing is impossible. Keep trying until you succeed and find happiness," now inspires me every day.

Looking around the house, filled with his photos, I realized I needed to continue living the lessons he taught me. This wasn't the end of his impact on me; it was just the beginning of a new chapter in continuing his legacy.

It's something I find myself thinking about more and more. It's like I'm being pulled back to those early days, to my childhood spent by his side, eager to rediscover how everything we shared shaped the person, who I am today.

Chapter 2:
Roots and Wings

Looking back, I see how my childhood, with all its challenges and joys, taught me so much. It showed me the value of hard work, the importance of family, and that it's okay to want more from life. My dreams started as just a tiny spark, but they grew, fueled by the love of my family and my determination to make something of myself. No matter where I go or what I do, I'll always carry these lessons with me. They're a big part of who I am and who I want to be.

Growing up in the bustling urban junction where Odisha meets Jharkhand, my life was set against a backdrop of cultural norms that often felt like they were from another era. In our little corner of the city, where houses were packed tightly together like books on a shelf, my family's home was no exception—small, crowded, but brimming with life.

I was that girl, the one who dared to dream big, towering dreams that often seemed at odds with the societal blueprint laid out for us. Tradition had its script—early marriages, predefined roles—but somewhere within me, there was this spark, this relentless flame that refused to flicker out, no matter how hard the winds of poverty blew.

My Family

Growing up, our family was a lively mix of different characters, each unique in their own right, but together, forming a picture of unity and love. Our house, though small, was always filled with the sounds of life—conversations, laughter, and the occasional argument, all of which echoed off the walls of our modest home.

My dad was the quiet backbone of our family. His job as a carpenter didn't just pay the bills; it was a testament to his skill and dedication. He would spend hours in his workshop, carefully shaping and crafting wood into furniture and other household items. Despite the simplicity of his work, it brought a deep sense of pride and security to our home.

His workshop was a place of magic for me. The sounds of sawing and hammering were the soundtrack of my childhood. I loved watching him work, seeing how he could take a piece of wood and turn it into something both beautiful and useful. It was from him I learned the value of hard work and the joy of creating something with your own hands.

Dad's way of showing care was through his actions. He might not have been big on words, but his efforts to provide for us spoke volumes. He worked tirelessly, often taking on extra jobs to ensure we had enough. His presence was a constant in our lives, offering stability and love in his quiet way.

He showed us what it meant to be committed and resilient. Even on his hardest days, he never complained.

Instead, he focused on solving whatever problem was in front of him, always with a calm and practical approach. This taught me not just to face challenges head-on but to do so with patience and perseverance.

Dad was more than a carpenter; he was my hero. Through his actions, he demonstrated the importance of dedication, kindness, and quiet strength. These lessons have stayed with me, shaping who I am today.

It was just me and my brother Gyan Babu at home. We didn't have a big, noisy family. But even though it was quiet, we had a strong bond. We shared everything, from small chores around the house to our hopes and worries.

Gyan Babu was more than a brother to me; he was my best friend. We talked about everything, laughed a lot, and supported each other no matter what. He was always there for me, giving advice or just listening when I needed someone to talk to.

Our home might have been quiet, but it was full of love and understanding between us. We didn't need anyone else to feel like a complete family. That closeness made us strong and kept us connected through all the ups and downs.

In this lively household, Mom and Dad were the anchors. But it was Grandpa, Mr. Perfect, who left the deepest imprint on my life. His presence was like a gentle but firm guiding hand. He wasn't just a relative; he was a mentor, a friend, and the wisest person I knew. His stories were not merely tales but life lessons wrapped in the guise of simple narratives. He taught us about respect, hard work, and the value of integrity without ever making us feel like we were in a classroom. His wisdom seemed to come from a place of deep understanding and experience, and his influence was the kind that shapes a person from the inside out.

Then there's the reality of poverty, a relentless shadow that seemed to follow us no matter where we went or what we did. Yet, here's what I've come to realise: it didn't get to define who we were or what we could become. Sure, poverty was part of our backdrop, an ever-present challenge that coloured our experiences. But it wasn't the author of our story. We were. Our dreams, our bonds, our resilience—that's what truly defined us. Poverty might have been a part of our life, but it was just that—apart. The real story was about us, how we faced it head-on, and how we didn't let it dictate our future.

The Monsoon Rain

That year, the rains came down harder than we'd ever seen, as if they had something against us. Our house, already shaky and worn, couldn't handle it. The roof started leaking, then just gave up, letting water flood in, making everything damp and cold.

This time, our usual struggles felt even heavier. We were always tight on money, but now, with the house needing fix-ups and food getting hard to find, things felt desperate. Nights were the worst. The darkness made the cold and hunger feel even more intense, and the sound of the rain seemed to mock us, laughing at our attempts to stay dry.

Food was the biggest worry. With everything soaking and the little money we had drying up fast, every meal became a question mark. We'd sit together, trying to stay warm, telling each other it would get better, but those words felt thin against the storm.

One such evening, when our stomachs were growling louder than the thunder outside, Grandpa, Mr. Perfect, arrived, unannounced but always welcomed. He stepped into our home—or what was left of it—with a look of concern that quickly masked over with his usual warm, reassuring smile. He could see the despair in our eyes, the defeat that we were too proud to voice. That night, none of us knew how to fill the gap of silence caused by hunger.

Seeing us huddled together, trying to find warmth and comfort in each other's presence, Mr. Perfect did something unexpected. He didn't try to fill our bellies with food we didn't have; instead, he filled our hearts with stories and lessons, a different kind of nourishment. We gathered around him, our bodies shivering, not just from the cold but also from the uncertainty of our situation.

In his hand, he held a piece of wood, once a part of our kitchen shelf, now just another casualty of the storm. "Look at this," he said, his voice calm and clear against the backdrop of the rain, "you might think it's finished, just a broken piece of what it used to be. But it's more than that." His eyes met each of us, making sure we were all with him on this journey of thought.

"This piece of wood," he continued, "it's a bit like us at this moment. Yes, it's broken, but that doesn't mean it's lost its value or potential. Think about it; with a little creativity and work, this could be part of something new, maybe even something better than it was before."

He paused, letting the idea sink in. "Being broken," he said, "doesn't mean we're defeated. It's a chance for us to come back stronger, to rebuild and reinvent ourselves. We're like this piece of wood, feeling a bit lost and shattered now, but within us, we have the strength to put ourselves back together, to emerge from this storm not just survived but thriving, stronger and more resilient than we ever imagined."

That night, even though our roof was leaking and we were all hungry, Grandpa gave us something very special. With just a broken piece of wood and his stories about getting through tough times, he showed us that the hard things we were going through now wouldn't stop us from having a good future. We all went to sleep feeling hopeful, filled with big dreams, knowing that no matter how bad the storm outside got, we had what it took inside us to get through it and come out even better.

This lesson from Grandpa stuck with me. It was like a light in the dark, pointing me to a future where being broken was just the start of becoming even stronger. As Grandpa always said, "In every broken piece, there's a story of resilience waiting to be told." That's something I'll never forget.

Chapter 3:
Dreams and Aspirations

On the platform, my heart is racing. I'm early for once, not because I might miss the train, but because I'm filled with so many emotions. Today, I carry more than just my luggage; I carry memories and lessons from the most important people in my life, especially my grandpa, Mr. Perfect. I check my watch, a habit I picked up from him, and can't help but smile. Mom jokes about my usual last-minute rushes, but today is different.

Mom looks both worried and cheerful as she tries to keep the mood light. "Seeing you here early, that's a first," she says with a smile, mixing concern with her usual humor. It's her way of showing she cares without making this goodbye too sad. I smile back, grateful for her efforts.

Behind her, my brother Gyan Babu stands quietly. In our family, we don't often show a lot of emotion; we're more subdued, showing care in our quiet ways. Gyan Babu being here without saying much says everything about his support.

"I'll miss you guys," I say, my words softer than I expect. "And please, make sure Dad's okay. You know his health hasn't been good." I try not to let my worry show too much.

Gyan Babu looks at me, and there's an understanding that doesn't need words. He might be the youngest, but sometimes he seems to understand me the most. "Look after them for me, okay?" I ask, my gaze shifting between him and Mom. The thought of leaving makes my chest tight, mixed with the excitement and fear of what lies ahead.

Leaving feels like their love is wrapping around me, like a hug that stays even when I walk away. "I'll make you all proud," I whisper, half to them, half to reassure myself, as I step onto the train. Settling into my seat, I feel a big responsibility resting on my shoulders—I'm carrying not just my bags but also Grandpa's dreams for me.

As the train starts, moving me further from home and closer to my exams, I think about my duty. "This one's for you, Grandpa," I say to myself, promising that I won't let him down. His belief in me doesn't weigh me down; it inspires me, gives me direction. Though he's not here right now because he's very ill, I carry his spirit, his advice, and his hopes for me as if they're right here in my suitcase.

Looking out the window as my hometown fades, I think about more than just the upcoming tests. I'm thinking about living up to the image Grandpa has of me, about fulfilling the dreams he and I share. It's a quiet moment, filled with anticipation and a bit of fear, but mostly, it's filled with determination.

I'm not just on a train to take my finals; I'm on a mission to prove to myself and to Grandpa that his faith in me was right. His stories and life lessons aren't just memories; they're the foundation of my ambitions, the reason I believe so deeply in making education accessible to everyone. As I sit here, the landscape rushing by, I'm not just Mamali going back to college; I'm Mamali on a mission, driven by the strongest influence in my life, ready to face whatever comes next.

Back to the Campus

After saying goodbye to my family, I felt all mixed up inside as I traveled back to college. I was really sad about Grandpa, Mr. Perfect, being so sick. It was hard to think about anything else. This made me late for Mr. Vaashi's class, which I usually try hard to avoid.

Rushing to the classroom, I felt bad when I saw the closed door.

Mr. Vaashi, my corporate communication teacher, has always been known for his strictness. Behind that serious front is a teacher who has greatly influenced my college experience. When I first arrived at college, struggling to find my feet, especially with English, Mr. Vaashi stepped in. It wasn't just about correcting my grammar or expanding my vocabulary; he showed me how effective communication could open doors, changing the way I expressed myself and connected with the world, which I felt was too far from me.

In many ways, he was more than just a teacher; he was a mentor who believed in my potential even when I doubted myself.

He never lets latecomers in. True to form, he saw me but shook his head, signalling I had to wait outside. Standing there, I felt sorry. Not just for being late, but for everything that seemed to be going wrong.

As I stood, lost in my thoughts, I noticed the watchman at the end of the corridor. He was talking to his son, a gentle but firm tone in his voice. It was hard not to overhear him convincing his son about something important, and their interaction, so full of care and guidance, reminded me of Grandpa. He had that same way of making you see sense, of guiding you without making you feel small.

After class, Mr. Vaashi stepped out and noticed me still standing there. He asked why I looked so disturbed. Reluctantly, I shared a bit about my recent loss and how it was affecting me. He listened quietly and then reminded me to focus on the upcoming exams. "These exams are important, not just for your grades, but for your future," he said, his voice softer than usual. "And don't forget to clear your fee dues," he added before walking away.

His words, though brief, reminded me that life had to go on. I had responsibilities and dreams to fulfil, not just for myself but for Grandpa too. He wouldn't have wanted me to get lost in my sorrow. So, with a deep breath, I promised myself to face what came with as much strength as I could muster.

Road to my Exams

With my exams fast approaching, I found myself buried in books, trying to soak up every bit of knowledge. Yet, a nagging worry haunted the back of my mind—my term fees were still unpaid. It was a significant hurdle I hadn't overcome, adding an extra layer of stress to the already intense exam prep.

One evening, I was sitting with my friend Deepthi in the campus corridor, who was knee-deep in her finance textbooks. She was always so focused, a trait I admired, especially with my thoughts scattered in a million directions.

Deepthi, on the other hand, is my senior, just about to finish her master's degree in finance. She's not just ambitious but deeply aware of societal issues. Her dream is to make a big difference, often talking about the importance of joining an NGO and helping the underprivileged. Deepthi is the kind of friend everyone needs in college—the one person I can be utterly open and vulnerable with.

I still remember our first real conversation. We were at the college cafeteria, both trying to study amidst the noise. She noticed the book I was struggling with and offered help without a second thought. "You know," she said, leaning over with a smile, "sometimes, all it takes is looking at the problem from a new angle." That day, we talked about everything from our courses to our dreams of making a difference in the world. It was easy and comfortable, and for the first time in a long while, I felt understood.

Our friendship grew from there, built on mutual respect and shared aspirations. Deepthi always encourages me to look beyond the college's walls, to see the bigger picture. "There's so much we can do, Mamali," she'd often say. "Education is just the beginning. Imagine the change we can bring, working with those who need it most."

It wasn't that I didn't believe in the goodness of serving others or the impact it could have. It's just that my immediate world, my family's needs, felt like the most pressing cause to dedicate my efforts to. Deepthi had great values, but it wasn't for me.

Opening up to her, I let out my fears, "I've been studying hard, Deepthi, but my fees... they're still pending. And honestly, I'm starting to question everything. What's the point of all this? After the exams, then what? With a degree in Commerce, I feel like I'm standing at a crossroads, and every path just seems... blank."

Deepthi looked up from her books, "Mamali," she said, her voice steady, "I get it, the uncertainty is scary. But think about how far you've come, and all the challenges you've faced. This degree, it's not just a piece of paper. It's a step towards your dreams, remember? The ones about making education accessible to everyone?"

"You're right," I replied, feeling a bit more grounded. "It's just... the fees. I need to figure that out first."

"We'll figure it out, together," Deepthi made me feel better, "You're not alone in this. And as for what comes after exams, let's take it one step at a time. You have dreams, big ones. This degree, your passion, it's going to lead you somewhere great. I believe in you."

Our conversation didn't magically solve my problems, but it gave me something just as valuable— hope and a reminder that I wasn't alone. Yes, the road ahead was uncertain, and the immediate hurdle of my unpaid fees loomed large.

The Main Day

Today was supposed to be just about exams, but there I was, stuck in the hallway, feeling like I couldn't move. My fees hadn't been paid yet, and it felt like this huge wall between me and walking into that exam room. I was pacing back and forth, trying to figure out what to do, when I saw the watchman's son coming my way.

He's this young kid, always running around the college, and today he looked right at me with a puzzled expression. You know how kids look at you when they can't quite figure something out? That's how he was looking at me.

"Why aren't you going into the exam?" he asked, his voice full of genuine wonder. He was just standing there, waiting for an answer, like he couldn't think of any reason why someone would miss an exam on purpose.

I didn't know how to explain to a kid about fees and money problems without making it sound like the world was ending. So, I just said, "It's a bit complicated. But what about you? Shouldn't you be in school right now?"

He scuffed his shoe against the ground, a bit shy all of a sudden. "We can't afford it right now," he said, looking up at me. It was like he thought it was no big deal, just something that happens.

That hit close to home. Here we were, him and me, not so different after all. We both knew what it was like when money got in the way of where you wanted to be.

I tried to smile, to show him it was okay, that we were both still standing there, doing just fine. "Yeah, I understand. Sometimes life gets in the way. But we keep going, right?"

He nodded, serious for such a young kid. "Yeah, we keep going."

And then off he went, probably to find another adventure in some corner of the college. I watched him go, thinking about what he said. It was simple, but maybe he was onto something. Maybe, no matter what, you just keep going.

Chapter 4:
Battles Within

Diving deeper into my past, I revisit the days of my past, a time when every step toward my dreams felt like walking against the current. Growing up in a village that lay on the serene but traditional borders of Odisha and Jharkhand, I was enveloped in a world where societal norms often dictated the path of a girl's life. Education for girls, though not entirely forbidden, was not encouraged beyond a certain point. It was an implicit boundary, one that few dared to challenge. Yet, inside me, there was a fire, a desire to learn, to know more, and to be more than just what was expected of me.

After school, walking home became a time for thinking about the future. We were waiting for exam results, which felt like forever. The results of our exams were still out, and that wait felt longer with each passing day. During this period something happened that made me think about the life I wanted versus the life the village expected of us girls.

My friend, Sanskriti, and I were sitting together outside, like we often did. Sanskriti had always talked about wanting to be a doctor. She was smart and more than capable. But that day, I noticed she seemed different, quieter.

"What's going on, Sanskriti? Thinking about college?" I tried to sound hopeful, knowing how much she wanted to pursue medicine.

She shook her head, looking down at her hands. *"No, Mamali. College isn't in the cards for me. My family... they're arranging my marriage."*

Hearing her say that hit me hard. "But all your plans to become a doctor... You can't just give up on that!"

Sanskriti gave a small, sad smile. *"It's not about what I want. You know how it is here. My parents have decided. It's not just me; it's how things are done in the village. Girls don't really go off to college. We get married."*

Her words made me angry and sad at the same time. Here was my friend, who had dreams and the determination to make them come true, being told her future was already decided for her.

"That's not fair, Sanskriti. You have endless potential. We can't let these outdated traditions dictate our lives."

She looked up, a bit of her old fire returning to her eyes. *"I wish things were different, Mamali. I do. But it's out of my hands."*

Our talk that day wasn't just a casual chat. It was a wake-up call for me. Seeing Sanskriti give up on her dreams because of our village's expectations made something clear to me. I didn't want that life. I wanted more. I craved more. I longed for education, for college, to prove that girls deserve equal opportunities.

"I'm not going to accept this, Sanskriti. I'm going to fight to go to college, to get that degree. Maybe if I do it, it'll show everyone that we can do more than just get married young…"

Sanskriti gave me a hopeful look. "I hope you make it, Mamali. If anyone can change things, it's you."

That conversation stayed with me. It wasn't just about me wanting to escape a fate similar to Sanskriti's. It became about challenging the very idea that girls couldn't pursue education or careers. I was determined to not only chase my dreams but to pave the way for other girls in my village to do the same. My path had taken on a new meaning. It wasn't just for me anymore; it was for all of us who wanted more from life than what was traditionally expected.

I Can't Study Anymore.

The day the school results came out was a day filled with mixed emotions. I had done well, better than I had dared hope, but the joy of my success was tinged with a deep sense of reality. Despite my achievements, the harsh truth was that college, the next step on my path to a better future, seemed just out of reach. The cost of further education was a barrier we couldn't overcome. My family, while proud of me, was also bound by the limitations of our circumstances.

My father, who had always quietly hoped I could break free from the constraints of our village's expectations, found himself at a crossroads. He never pushed me towards marriage, unlike the norm in our village, because he saw the spark in me, the desire to learn and grow. But wishing for something and having the means to achieve it are two different things. Our reality was stark—we couldn't afford college.

Feeling like I was walking with empty hands of hope, and a heavy heart accompanying every step. I couldn't bear the thought of all my dreams, all my hard work, ending here. In a moment of seeking solace and perhaps looking for answers, I decided to visit Mr. Perfect, my grandfather. He was always wise and helpful to me. Even when I felt very sad, he showed me new ways.

As I made my way to his place, the journey felt different this time. It wasn't just a visit; it was a search for clarity, for strength to accept my reality and yet find a way to keep my dreams alive. Mr. Perfect had always encouraged me to pursue education, to aim for the stars, and now, faced with the possibility of my journey ending prematurely, I needed his wisdom more than ever.

Getting back home, everything felt familiar and that brought some comfort to my unsettled heart. His warm smile welcomed me, and he could tell something was bothering me just by looking into my eyes. Sitting down beside him, the words spilled out. I told him about my results, about the college dilemma, and the pressure of village expectations weighing heavily on me.

Listening quietly, Mr. Perfect took my hands in his. *"Life,"* he began, *"is filled with challenges, but it's also filled with opportunities. Sometimes, the path we're meant to take isn't the one we've always envisioned. Your education doesn't have to end here. There are ways, ways that we can explore together. And marriage, if and when it happens, should be on your terms, when you're ready, not because it's expected."*

Mrs. Perfect

Walking around the village, feeling a mix of hope and confusion from my talk with Grandpa, I ended up near the fields where my grandma was. She was busy with the farm work, looking as strong and determined as always. Seeing her, I felt a bit of my worry slip away, replaced by a curiosity to hear her take on everything.

I went up to her, and we started chatting. Somehow, we got onto the topic of how tough things can be in the village, especially with how people treat you based on things like your skin color or if your family doesn't have much money. I couldn't help but spill out my own worries. "Why does it feel like I'm always on the outside looking in? Just because we're poor, doesn't mean I don't want the same things as other kids," I said, feeling that familiar sting of unfairness.

Grandma stopped her work and looked at me, her eyes kind but serious. She shared something I hadn't heard before. She told me about her own dreams when she was younger. She wanted to be a teacher more than anything. But back then, people thought a woman's place wasn't in a classroom, at least not in front of it. And just like me, she wondered why she couldn't have what she dreamed of.

"But you know what?" she said, wiping her hands on her saree, "I was lucky. When I married your grandpa, I found someone who saw me for me. He knew about my dream and he supported it. He's the reason I eventually got to stand in front of a classroom, to teach."

I looked at her, and really saw her, in her teacher's clothes, ready to head off to school. It hit me then how much she'd managed to achieve, despite everything.

Just then, Grandpa came out, a smile on his face. He had news. Somehow, he'd managed to secure me a spot in college. It wasn't about him being well-off; we all knew that wasn't the case. But Grandpa has always been rich in ways that mattered more—rich in heart, rich in believing in us.

Hearing that, standing there with Grandma, it all felt a bit surreal. My worries about being different, about not fitting in because of where we came from or how little we had, seemed to fade a bit. Here were two people who'd faced their own battles, their own moments of feeling out of place, and yet, they'd carved out a life full of love and understanding. And now, they were doing everything they could to help me chase my own dreams, just like they had.

Present Day

Back at college, outside the exam hall, my heart was racing for a whole different reason. The fees situation had me frozen in place, unable to step inside and take the exams that meant everything to me. Just when I felt like giving up, someone tapped my shoulder. Turning around, I found our office clerk with a smile, "Your fees have been cleared. You can go in for your exam now."

For a moment, I just stared at him, not fully grasping his words. Cleared? How? My family had been stretching every rupee till it screamed. Rushing into the exam hall, my mind was a whirlwind. Who could have...? Then it hit me – Grandma. It had to be. She knew how much this meant to me, and knew about my dreams and the obstacles in my way.

Once I was seated, ready with my pen poised over the paper, the realization slowly sank in. Grandma had done it. She'd found a way to pay my fees. This was more than just money for exams; it was her belief in me, her way of pushing me forward when I felt like I was at a dead end. I remembered our talks, her stories of past struggles, her sacrifices, and how she always believed things could get better.

That moment wasn't just about taking an exam anymore. It was about everything Grandma and Grandpa had taught me, about overcoming challenges and keeping faith in your dreams. Knowing Grandma believed in me enough to do this filled me with a strength I didn't know I had.

As I began to answer the questions, each word I wrote felt like a step closer to my dreams, a promise to Grandma that her belief in me wasn't misplaced. This exam turned into more than just a test of what I'd learned in class; it was proof that with support, love, and a bit of stubbornness, we can face our biggest challenges.

Leaving the exam hall, I wasn't just relieved it was over. I was determined, determined to make Grandma proud, to show her that her sacrifice wouldn't be wasted. I was going to finish college, no matter what it took, because now I knew for sure I wasn't doing it alone.

Chapter 5:
Financial Turmoil

Right after I handed in my last exam, I felt a huge sigh of relief. But that good feeling didn't last long. Almost right away, I started worrying about what I was supposed to do next. Jobs weren't exactly lined up and waiting for me, and that hit me pretty hard, I started stressing about what to do next since I didn't have a job lined up. It felt like I was at a fork in the road, had to choose between studying more or starting work, but I didn't know which path to take.

Alone in my room, surrounded by silence, I kept turning those options over in my mind. Thinking about studying more seemed exciting because it meant learning new things that could open up doors for the future. But the idea of jumping back into all that studying without a clear goal scared me too. Then there was the job option. It made sense because I could really use the money, but I was scared I'd end up in a job that didn't lead anywhere, just stuck.

I kept swinging back and forth, unable to settle. The more I thought about it, the more overwhelmed I felt. Both choices had good and bad sides, and I just couldn't figure out which way to lean. It was a lot to think about, and I wasn't sure which path was the right one for me.

Weeks passed, and I had lots of interviews, feeling both hopeful and anxious. I tried to move past the uncertainty, believing that one of these chances would be my big break. Each interview felt like a step towards a new opportunity, a chance to find my way after college. But as time went on, the excitement faded, and waiting for responses and facing rejections became harder.

During that period, I spent my days chasing job opportunities and waiting for my phone to ring, but it stayed silent. The quietness from potential employers seemed to grow louder every day, reminding me of the uncertainty that lay ahead.

In the midst of ups and downs, I received calls from my grandpa, Mr. Perfect. His calls always brought joy to my week, filled with tales, wisdom, and shared laughter as always brightened my day.

One afternoon, feeling particularly low, I noticed the watchman's son playing alone outside. On a whim, I asked, "Hey, do you want to go get some ice cream with me?" his face lit up with excitement. Together, we headed out for a sweet treat.

As we sat at the ice cream shop, I found myself talking to him. "I've been looking for a job since I finished my exams," I said. "But nothing's working out. I thought I'd have everything figured out by now, but I feel more confused than ever." I wasn't sure why I was telling him all this, but it just came out.

He was halfway through his ice cream cone, listening intently. Then, he said something that caught me off guard. "But isn't it okay not to have everything figured out?" he said, pausing to think. "It's like this ice cream. There are so many flavors I haven't tried. I wouldn't know which ones I like unless I try them, right? Maybe it's the same with jobs and… stuff."

We continued chatting, him with his childlike wisdom and me, surprised by how much sense he was making. Walking back from the ice cream shop, feeling a bit lighter thanks to the watchman's son's unexpected wisdom, my phone rang. It was Mr. Perfect. The moment I heard his voice, serious and filled with concern, my heart sank. "You need to come home," he said urgently. "It's your dad. He's very unwell."

That call felt like a sharp turn in the road I was on. Suddenly, all my worries about jobs and what I was doing with my life seemed small compared to this. My dad was sick, really sick, and that meant everything was about to change.

When I got home, I saw firsthand just how bad things were. Dad was ill, too ill to work, and without his income, we were quickly sliding into financial trouble. It wasn't just about making ends meet anymore; it was about how we were going to afford his treatment on top of everything else.

This crisis hit us hard, shaking the very foundation of our family. For me, it brought a whole new layer of uncertainty about my future. My education, the dreams I had of doing more, getting a better job, suddenly felt like they were slipping through my fingers. The idea of further studies, or even just focusing on finding a job, seemed impossible now. I needed to be here, with my family, trying to figure out how we were going to get through this tough time.

Dad's condition went from bad to worse in what felt like moments. The doctor said it was a severe lung infection that needed surgery, and soon. That news hit us like a thunderbolt. With Dad being the main breadwinner for our family, his illness didn't just mean we were worried sick about him; it meant our already tight finances were stretched to the breaking point.

We were living in a constant state of poverty, and with Dad's illness, it felt like we had hit rock bottom. There was no money coming in, and the little we had saved was quickly eaten up by hospital bills and medicine. Hope seemed like a luxury we couldn't afford. Our lives had shrunk to a cycle of home and hospital visits, a routine that was as exhausting emotionally as it was physically.

That evening at home really stuck with me. Gyan had been doing so much. He had stopped attending school and even quit his job to help out, all because we were going through such a tough time. When he returned home that day, I could see the toll it had taken on him. He looked exhausted and troubled.

Our house felt unusually silent, with Dad still in the hospital. Gyan usually makes jokes, trying to cheer everyone up, but that day, he was just quiet. He hadn't eaten much, and I could sense his hunger, not just for food but perhaps maybe tired from everything that was happening.

I felt really bad seeing him like this. My brother had given up a lot for me and our family. It made me feel guilty, knowing all he was sacrificing. Gyan would probably say it's no big deal, that he's just doing what family does for each other. But that doesn't make me feel any less grateful or worried about him.

So, I got up to make something to eat, just something simple. But even with the two of us there, the house felt too silent. It wasn't just quiet; it felt like the silence was filled with all the stress and worry we were both feeling but not talking about. That silence made everything seem even harder, like it was emphasising just how much we missed Dad and how much everything had changed for us.

Beside My Father

Staying back with Dad in the hospital became my new reality. Days and nights blended into one long vigil by his bedside. The hospital smell, a mix of disinfectant and sickness, started to make me nauseous. It seemed to cling to everything—my clothes, my hair, even my skin. That scent served as a constant reminder of our situation, of the powerlessness that comes with watching a loved one suffer without being able to help.

The hospital corridors, the waiting rooms, and the endless hours spent hoping for good news became the backdrop of my life.

I remember it clearly, a day with a wind that felt significant. Gyan Babu and I were outside the hospital when a nurse hurried out, looking worried. "Quickly," she said, "Your dad... he's having trouble breathing." Panic surged as we rushed inside, our hearts pounding.

Outside the emergency ward, watching doctors come and go, I felt the seriousness of the situation. Mr. Perfect, Grandpa, was on his way, having decided to sell our last piece of land to pay for Dad's surgery. The wind seemed to echo the turmoil inside me.

As I stood there, the wind howling around us, fear consumed me. The thought of losing Dad, of not having him around in a future where everything was okay, where we were all happy together, was unbearable. I imagined us laughing together in better times, free from hospitals and worries about money or health. The fear of that dream never coming true squeezed my heart.

Mr. Perfect arrived, his face a mix of resolve and sadness. The land, our last tangible asset, was gone, but in its place was hope for Dad's recovery. Waiting outside the emergency ward, with the wind as my only company, I realized that no matter what happened, we had each other. The fear, the hope, the sacrifices— it all blended into a sharp focus on what mattered most: family, love, and the bonds that hold us together through the hardest times.

During Dad's surgery, tension hung heavy in the air. Grandpa and I found a quiet spot nearby to wait. Unable to hold back tears, I broke down. The worry for Dad overwhelmed me. What struck me the most was seeing Grandpa so shaken. He's always been our rock, but at that moment, he looked truly scared.

"I can't bear to lose him," Grandpa whispered. His worry weighed heavily on me. He wasn't just afraid for Dad; he was afraid for all of us, for our entire family. Seeing Grandpa, usually so strong, look so helpless made me realise something crucial. It was my turn to be the pillar of strength for him.

"Dad's a fighter. Remember how he always tells us to never give up? Now, it's our turn to have faith in him, to believe he won't give up."

Grandpa nodded slowly, absorbing my words. "You're right," he said after a pause. "Your dad has always been the one to keep us moving forward, to show us the brighter side of things. But it's tough, you know, seeing him like this and feeling so powerless."

I reached out and held his hand. "I know, Grandpa. It's scary. But we're not facing this alone. We have each other, and we'll get through it together. We'll be here for Dad, just like he's always been supporting us."

There was a long pause as we both sat there, lost in our thoughts. Finally, Grandpa squeezed my hand back. "Thank you," he said, his voice stronger now. "I needed to hear that. It's easy to forget, in moments like these, that we have each other to lean on."

"We won't let Dad down," I added, feeling a new resolve settle over me. "And we won't let each other down either. We're a family, and we'll face whatever comes our way together."

Grandpa smiled at me, a small but genuine smile. "That's the spirit," he said. "Your dad would be proud of you, of how strong you're being right now."

We just sat there together, not saying much, but it felt like we were really supporting each other. It made me see that even the strongest people can feel scared and that it's okay. When it comes to family, we all want to do whatever we can to help, even if we're scared on the inside.

Waiting for the surgery to end felt like an eternity. But Grandpa and I held onto hope, waiting together for the news that Dad was okay. It showed me how much our family means to each other. No matter how tough things get, we stick together, hoping for the best. That hope is what keeps us going, believing that soon, we'll all be reunited, happy and healthy.

Chapter 6:
The Pillars of Strength

After the operation, Dad had to stay in bed for a long time. The doctors said he needed a lot of rest and care to get better. That meant I had to stay at home to take care of him. Suddenly, everything else – my education, the job search, all the plans I had – just had to wait. Being there for my dad was the most important thing.

As time passed, days turned into weeks, and weeks into months, my world revolved around Dad's care. I ensured he took his medicine, assisted him in moving around when possible, and simply stayed by his side, providing companionship. Although it was tough witnessing his weakness, I understood his dependence on me and was committed to supporting him through it all.

During that period, school and job hunting hardly crossed my mind. It's not that I abandoned my dreams or goals, but they lost their sense of urgency. Dad's well-being consumed my thoughts entirely. Every day was dedicated to him and our family, striving to navigate through this challenging phase together.

It was tough. Some days, I felt like everything was too much, and I doubted if things would ever go back to how they were. But then I'd see Dad's determination to get better, and it gave me the courage to keep pushing forward. If he was fighting, I knew I had to fight alongside him, even if it meant things were different now.

In the end, family comes first, and being with Dad was where I needed to be. Every day felt like a cycle of tasks, a list of chores to complete. Yet, amidst the routine, there was a calmness in this chapter of my life that I hadn't felt before

In the beginning, after Dad was discharged from the hospital, we had a lot of visitors. Relatives, friends, and neighbours all came by to check on him and offer support. But as weeks went by, the visits became less frequent. Gradually, the house felt emptier, and the lively atmosphere of those initial days faded into a deep silence

Taking care of Dad as he recovered from a serious illness meant that every meal and medication time required careful attention. He relied on me for everything, and although I was happy to assist him, the reality was draining. There were medications to sort out, doctor's appointments to remember, and the constant concern about hospital expenses hanging over us.

The silence in the house wasn't just physical; it seemed to permeate everything. Conversations mostly revolved around Dad's health or household tasks, with laughter becoming rare and discussions about the future avoided. It felt as though the illness had sucked the life out of our home, leaving behind a hollow feeling.

Caring for Dad, witnessing his struggle to recover, constantly reminded me of life's fragility. In the moments of quietness between us, I often pondered how much things had changed. Our once bustling home now echoed with the solitude of our altered reality.

The Quiet Fight

After spending the entire day at the hospital, the tension and worry clinging to me like a second skin, I walked into a house charged with frustration. Gyan Babu, usually the calm one, was pacing back and forth, his voice raised in anger. I was taken aback; this was not the homecoming I had expected.

"What's going on, Gyan? Why are you shouting?" I asked, barely getting my shoes off.

"It's everything! It's just too much. I can't deal with this silence, this... doing nothing!" he exploded. His words, so full of raw emotion, struck a nerve, and before I knew it, I was yelling back.

"We are all struggling here, Gyan! Do you think this is easy for me? For any of us?" My own pent-up frustrations and fears were bubbling to the surface, and I couldn't hold them back.

The shouting match was abruptly cut short by Mom's calm but firm voice. *"Enough, both of you!"* She looked at us with a mixture of sadness and understanding. We fell silent, the tension still hanging heavy in the air.

Sitting down at the kitchen table, Mom looked at us. *"This is our new reality,"* she began softly. *"We have to accept it. With no income coming in, it's going to be hard. Empty stomachs, yes, will lead to misunderstandings, to anger. But we can't let that tear us apart."*

Mom didn't try to comfort us with hopeful words like she usually might. She didn't say anything at all. She just sat there, looking... I don't know, kind of empty. Like she was miles away from us, lost in her thoughts about everything that was going wrong.

It was hard to see her like that. Mom's always been the one to keep us all together, to find something positive to say no matter how bad things got.

Later, Gyan came to find me. I was sitting alone, trying to process everything. He sat next to me in silence for a moment, not saying a word.

"Do you remember how we used to be, Didi? Even when things weren't great, we had Dad keeping us together. We faced everything as a family,"* he started, *"But now, it feels like we're all in our own corners. It's making me feel more alone than I've ever felt."*

"I don't like seeing you like this," he continued, reaching for my hand. *"You've always been the one with dreams, with plans to do something big. And not everyone has that kind of strength, that kind of resilience. I'm proud of you, Didi. I'll always be."*

Tears filled my eyes as I witnessed Gyan, my younger brother, showing a maturity beyond his years.

"I want you to go and follow your path. Don't worry about us here. I promise I'll take care of everything at home,"

When Gyan said he'd take care of everything, I felt something change inside me. We hugged a strong hug that meant more than any words could. *"Thanks, Gyan. That really means a lot,"* I managed to say, filled with thanks and feeling a bit more hopeful.

What Gyan did wasn't just about saying it's okay for me to do what I want; it was about him stepping up. It showed me a new side of him. In that tough time, we understood each other. It reminded us that we're there for each other, no matter what.

My Pillar

While all of this is happening, I couldn't help but notice Dad. He wasn't joining in our conversations but was observing everything with a look that spoke volumes. In his eyes, there was this mix of helplessness and guilt, as if he was silently blaming himself for the situation we were all in.

Dad had always been the backbone of our family, the one who worked hard to make sure we had everything we needed. Now, seeing him bedridden and unable to contribute, I could sense he felt like he was more of a burden than a help. It was a hard realisation, and he didn't voice these thoughts to anyone, but his expressions gave him away.

I saw it in the way he watched us from his corner of the room. There was this sadness, a kind of resignation as if he believed he was the cause of our struggles. It was clear he thought that because he couldn't provide for us or take care of us the way he used to, he was adding to our problems. This unspoken feeling of guilt seemed to weigh on him, adding to the physical battle he was already fighting.

Dad didn't say anything about it, but I knew. I could see it every time our eyes met, every time he watched Gyan and me discussing how to manage our next steps. It broke my heart to see him like this, to see him feel like he was anything less than the hero we always knew him to be.

———

One night, everyone was asleep, and suddenly, Dad started coughing really badly. It wasn't a little cough; it went on and on, and he just couldn't stop. We all woke up and ran to him, scared and trying to figure out what to do. Seeing Dad like that, struggling to breathe, made us all worried. It took a while, but finally, the coughing started to slow down, and Dad could breathe more easily again.

After things calmed down a bit, and everyone else went back to bed, I couldn't make myself leave Dad's side. I was too scared that it might happen again, and I wanted to be there just in case. So, I stayed, sitting next to his bed, watching him sleep. I listened to every breath he took, making sure he was breathing okay.

I felt so many things. I was scared, of course, but also really wanted to be there for him, to make sure he was safe. It was a simple thing, just sitting there, but it felt important.

After a while, Dad woke up and noticed me sitting by his bed. He looked a bit surprised and asked, *"What are you still doing up? You should be getting some sleep."*

I just smiled at him and said, *"I wanted to make sure you were okay. Couldn't sleep anyway."*

Dad shook his head, a faint smile on his face. *"I'm fine, really. You kids worry too much,"* he tried to reassure me.

"I never thought I'd be the one keeping everyone awake at night. Look at me, making a fuss and causing trouble."

I quickly said, *"You're not causing any trouble, Dad. We're just a bit scared when things like this happen. It's all new to us."*

He chuckled softly, trying to lighten the mood. *"Well, I must say, it's a strange feeling, being taken care of like this. I'm supposed to be the strong one, remember?"*

I laughed with him, happy to see him in good spirits. *"We all take turns being strong,"* I told him. *"Right now, it's our turn to be strong for you."*

We continued talking, the conversation flowing easily. Despite the situation, there was comfort in just sharing these moments, talking about everything and nothing. It was nice, being there with him, making the night feel a little less heavy.

Dad then asked about Mr. Perfect, curious how he was handling everything. I shared with him how

Grandpa had been worried, how he even had tears in his eyes. It was a rare sight, seeing him so overwhelmed.

Dad nodded, understandingly. "It's funny, isn't it? Every father turns into a kid themselves when their loved ones are in trouble. My father was the same with me," he said softly. "He always stood by me, no matter what. And now, I want to do the same for you. I want to see you happy, achieving everything you've ever wanted."

He paused for a moment, looking straight at me. "That's why, my dear, I want you to go. Follow your dreams. Don't stay stuck here, worrying about me. You were meant for bigger things than this," Dad urged. "You shouldn't be in a nutshell here with me. Spread your wings and fly. I'll be okay. I want you to reach for the places you've always desired to go."

As Dad fell asleep while we were talking, I stayed by his side, lost in thought. The love and support of my family, through all these hard times, truly was my biggest strength. It was a mix of feelings - sadness at the thought of leaving, yet a deep sense of gratitude and inspiration from knowing I had his blessing.

Sitting there in the quiet, watching him sleep peacefully, I realised just how much my family's support meant to me. They were my pillars of strength, each in their way. Mom, with her quiet resilience, Gyan with his understanding and encouragement, and Dad, with his tireless belief in my dreams. They created a strong circle of love around me, reminding me that no matter where life led, I had a stable base to return to.

Stepping into the world with my family's love and blessings made chasing my dreams feel achievable. It wasn't just about my success; it was about honoring their sacrifices and belief in me. Their strong support comforted me and drove me forward, showing me that together, we could overcome any challenge.

Chapter 7:
Turning Point

Riding back to the city on the bus, I was surrounded by all sorts of noise. Some friends were laughing, talking loudly about their summer break. Not far from me, a husband and wife were arguing over something small, their voices sharp and frustrated. The conductor was busy, moving through the packed bus, collecting fares and handing out tickets, all while trying not to bump into anyone. Meanwhile, the driver was focused on the road, steering us through stretches of greenery outside. The bus's speakers were playing a lively Hindi song, which felt oddly out of place with the mood inside the bus.

Sitting there, I couldn't help but watch all these people around me. It made me think about my own life and everything happening at home.

On that bus ride, it struck me how all these stories and scenes had always been there, part of the backdrop of daily life that I hadn't really paid attention to before. Everyone had their own reasons for being here, their own goals and dreams. It made me ask myself, "What's mine?"

Back to Base

Back in the city, I knew I couldn't just spend my days searching for jobs like before. There was no room for confusion or waiting around this time. I needed to earn some money, not just for myself, but to help out with Dad's medical bills and everything else at home. Depending on my family for support wasn't an option; they needed my help too.

Walking through the crowded city streets, everyone seemed to be in a rush, each person caught up in their own daily race. It was a hustle everywhere I looked – people going to work, running errands, or just trying to make it through another day. This hustle of the city, it was like a mirror to the urgency I felt inside.

This wasn't just about finding a job anymore; it was about finding a way to contribute, to lighten the load on my family in any way I could. The weight of our financial situation was pressing down harder than ever, and I couldn't stand by, watching from the sidelines.

So, I started thinking about what I could do right now, with the skills and resources I had.

That's when I ran into Sanskriti. We hadn't seen each other in a while, but she was just the person I needed to see at that moment. We decided to catch up over a cup of coffee.

As we sat down, I shared with her my thoughts about starting tutoring. I was still turning the idea over in my mind, unsure about the practicalities of it all.

Sanskriti listened, then smiled. *"Remember back in school? You were always the one explaining things to the rest of us. You had a way of making complicated stuff seem easy,"* she said.

I nodded, recalling those days. *"Yeah, I remember. But that was school. This is different,"* I replied, the uncertainty clear in my voice.

"But why does it have to be? You were great at teaching even then. I always understood things better when you explained them," Sanskriti encouraged. *"You have a gift, and now, more than ever, you should use it."*

Her words made me think. I had always enjoyed those moments back in school, the satisfaction of helping someone understand something they'd been struggling with. It was rewarding in a way I hadn't really acknowledged until now.

"And besides, you said it yourself, you need to do something that doesn't depend on waiting for opportunities to come your way. Tutoring could be it. You could start small, maybe with the kids in the neighbourhood," Sanskriti suggested, her eyes lighting up with the idea.

Her suggestion sparked something in me. It made sense, a lot of sense. Tutoring didn't just align with my skills and passion for teaching; it was something tangible I could start on my own.

As we finished our coffee and started to part ways, Sanskriti's question hung in the air, *"So, where will you start?"*

Where indeed? Her question wasn't just about the logistics of finding students or setting up as a tutor. It was bigger than that. It was about taking that first step towards a new chapter, one where I could potentially turn my passion into something that could support my family and me.

It started with AMAR

Meeting Amar, the watchman's son, again felt like a sign. Oh, I forgot to mention his name earlier. He was curious, always asking questions, and once he asked me, "If you can learn so much in college, why do I need to go to school?" His question was simple but got me thinking about how much guidance he needed. Amar was bright and eager to learn, but his family's financial situation made it tough for him to get the education he deserved.

I saw an opportunity there, not just for Amar but for myself too. I decided to help him, to tutor him. I told his dad, "I want to help Amar with his studies. You don't have to pay me anything. I'm looking for a place to start, and helping Amar seems like the right thing to do." His father was taken aback by the offer but deeply grateful.

Amar was a kid with a lot of potential, a "small bundle with big perspectives," as I came to see him. Tutoring Amar wasn't just about imparting maths or science lessons; it was about unlocking a world of opportunities for both of us. For Amar, it meant the opportunity to pursue his dreams and escape the grip of poverty. For me, it marked the beginning, my initial foray into the realm of teaching that I had long contemplated but had struggled to enter.

This decision to help Amar was more than just an act of kindness; it was the beginning of my journey into tutoring. Amar became my first student, a way for me to test the waters of this new path I was considering. It felt good, right, to be using my knowledge and passion for teaching to make a difference in someone's life, especially someone as eager and deserving as Amar.

Starting to tutor Amar felt right, and our rapport was surprisingly good. He was eager to learn, and I found real joy in teaching him. However, as rewarding as it was to see his progress, it wasn't the complete solution to my own problems. Despite this, something special was happening throughout our sessions.

One day, after we finished a lesson, Amar turned to me with a sincerity in his eyes I hadn't seen before. *"You're doing so much for me,"* he said, his voice full of genuine gratitude. *"It makes me believe more in life. I promise I'm going to study hard, get a good job, and take care of my family, just like you're helping us."*

Then he asked, *"Why do you look sad sometimes?"* It caught me off guard. Amar, this young kid with so much of life ahead of him, noticed the weight I was carrying, the struggles I tried to hide while I was with him.

It felt like a moment to be honest, to share a bit of my own world with him. Despite his young age, Amar had this understanding and empathy that went beyond his years. So, I told him about my struggles, the pressure of needing to support my family, and how tutoring wasn't just a job for me but a way to make a difference, like I hoped to do for him.

Amar listened quietly, not interrupting, just giving me space to talk. It was comforting, almost as if he understood me better than anyone else had lately. His silent support felt like an anchor, reminding me that sometimes, sharing your worries can lighten your load, even if just a little.

I explained to Amar, *"I'm pushing you to aim high, to believe in bigger things for yourself because that's what Mr. Perfect did for me."* His curiosity piqued, Amar asked, *"Why do you call him Mr. Perfect?"*

I smiled with a hint of fondness, *"I'll tell you later,"* *I said, leaving the story for another time.*

The Sun Rises

This time of day, with the sun setting, had become our regular slot for English lessons. The terrace, usually a quiet spot in my home, turned into our little classroom each evening. I liked teaching here; the open sky and the fading daylight created a calm, focused atmosphere.

When Amar didn't show up as expected, my initial worry quickly turned to frustration. punctuality was something I valued, especially when planning our lessons around the daylight hours we had left. Eventually, Amar rushed in, a bit breathless and clearly late. Despite my relief at seeing him, I couldn't hold back my scolding. He needed to understand the value of time, especially in learning.

"We've got English today, Amar. You know how important these lessons are," I reminded him, trying to shift the focus back to why we were here. Amar nodded, English was a subject he was particularly keen on mastering. He saw it as a key to unlocking many doors in the future, and I was determined to help him open as many as possible.

But then, something unexpected happened. As I was teaching Amar, correcting his sentences and encouraging him to try again, the door opened. One by one, several kids from Amar's neighbourhood began to get in. They were all like Amar in some way, coming from underprivileged backgrounds, their faces marked with a mix of curiosity and hesitation.

Amar, seeing my surprise, explained, *"I told them about you, about how you're helping me. They want to learn too."* He said some families could afford to pay a little for their lessons. It wasn't much, but it would help, he assured me.

My small terrace, usually so quiet and reserved for Amar's lessons, suddenly felt like a vibrant classroom. As more kids found spots to sit, some on the floor, others pulling up whatever makeshift seats they could find, I felt a wave of emotions. Overwhelmed, yes, but also touched by their eagerness to learn and Amar's initiative to bring them to me.

So, I continued the class, now not just teaching Amar but a group of eager young minds. My lesson plan for the day quickly adapted from one-on-one tutoring to a group session, discussing basic English phrases, correcting pronunciations, and encouraging questions. The terrace, usually just a simple space in my home, transformed into a place of learning, of connection.

When I asked the kids what they wanted to learn, their answer came in a unanimous shout: "English!" At first, I was surprised. I thought Amar's interest in English was unique to him. Curious, I asked them why they were all so eager to learn this particular language. Their responses opened my eyes. They felt that not speaking English well put them at a disadvantage, that it somehow placed others who spoke it fluently above them. This wasn't just about communication; it was about equality, about feeling confident and respected.

This conversation reminded me of something Mr. Perfect once said. He believed that language should never be a barrier or a symbol of superiority. It's a tool, a bridge that connects us to others. "Unless you understand the language, you can't fully understand the person speaking it," he would say. This wasn't about mastering English to fit in or to claim some kind of social standing. It was about empowering these kids to express themselves clearly, to share their thoughts and ideas without hesitation, and to engage with the world on equal footing.

Teaching them English, then, became more than just lessons in grammar and vocabulary. It was about instilling confidence, about showing them that their voices mattered. I wanted them to know that being able to communicate effectively means being understood, being seen, and, most importantly, treating and being treated as equals.

Reflecting on Mr. Perfect's influence, I realised he was like the compass that guided me through every step of this journey. His lessons went beyond academics; they were about life, understanding, and connecting with others on a deeper level. Now, as I stood on the terrace surrounded by these keen young minds, it felt as though Mr. Perfect's spirit was right there with us, guiding each lesson, each word I spoke.

"Sharing knowledge multiplies its impact. When we teach others, we not only enlighten their paths but also illuminate our own."

Chapter 8:
A Passion Ignited

Teaching the kids on our rooftop has turned into the best part of my day. Every evening, as the sun begins to set, filling the sky with colors, the rooftop comes alive with the chatter and laughter of the kids coming to learn English. It's become something I look forward to, a time filled with joy and a lot of learning, not just for the kids but for me too.

We've had our share of funny moments. Like the time Arjun thought he could impress everyone with a cartwheel and ended up in a heap on the mat I'd put down, thankfully not hurt. We all couldn't stop laughing, Arjun included. Then there's Ravi, whose writing nobody can read, not even him. We joke that he's invented a new language, and now we're all trying to learn it together. Sohan tries so hard with his English, mixing up words in ways that make us laugh until our sides hurt, but he keeps trying, and that's what matters.

When the lessons end and it's time for everyone to go home, the rooftop goes quiet. I stand there for a while, watching the kids leave, their voices fading away. It's in these quiet moments that I really take in what we're doing here. It's more than just learning English;

it's about coming together, supporting each other, and growing.

I often find myself thinking about each of them as they leave, about their mischief and their efforts. There's something special about teaching them, about the connections we're building. Like when Arjun fell, we all felt it, but we also all laughed together. When we try to decipher Ravi's writing, it's a challenge we take on as a group. And hearing Sohan's jumbled English reminds us all that making mistakes is part of learning.

After everyone's gone, the rooftop is peaceful. I stay up there a bit, thinking about the day, about Mr. Perfect and how he'd love to see what's happening here. This isn't just about English; it's about giving these kids confidence, showing them, they're valued, and helping them see that they can achieve whatever they set their minds to.

As I look out over the quiet rooftop, I feel really thankful for this chance to teach, to make even a small difference in their lives. It's these moments, these lessons, that remind me why I started this in the first place. And as the last light of the day fades, I'm already looking forward to tomorrow, to another evening filled with learning, laughter, and a bit of mischief on our rooftop.

Amidst the busy days and the lively lessons on the rooftop, I found myself drawn to a new, quiet hobby: writing poetry. It became my way of capturing the thoughts swirling in my head, the laughter of the kids, and the lessons we shared. My poetry was a patchwork of the days' moments, stitched together with words inspired by our experiences.

Here's a Piece I Wrote, Reflecting on those Rooftop Gatherings:

Today's entry feels like a song,
Sung by hearts young and strong.
On our rooftop, under the fading light,
We learn, we laugh, we take flight.

Arjun leaps, lands with a thud,
We cheer, he grins, covered in mud.
"Phir se!" they cry, with joy they beam,
In their eyes, the spark of a dream.

Ravi's pen dances, a wild spree,
Lines and loops, free as can be.
His words, a puzzle we love to solve,
In every mistake, our world evolves.

Sohan's English, a delightful mix,
His efforts, our daily fix.
"Koshish kar," I gently guide,
His progress, our collective pride.

This journal, a keeper of days so bright,
Of moments that turn darkness into light.
Here, in these simple words, I find,
The echoes of their laughter, forever entwined.

With each day, a new story to tell,
In this corner of the world where we dwell.
Our lessons, more than language, a bond,
A promise of tomorrows, fond.

So here I write, under the sky's vast dome,
Of the rooftop where hearts find a home.
In these moments, small yet profound,
A universe of understanding, unbound.

It was a way to hold onto the feelings, the breakthroughs, and even the challenges. Each verse reminded me of the impact these kids had on me, and perhaps, the impact I had on them. This newfound love for poetry wasn't just a hobby; it became a vital part of who I am, a way to express the deeper connections formed on that rooftop, under the vast sky.

Sohan, The Author

That particular day on the rooftop, as the evening approached and the sky began to change colours, I decided to steer our English lesson in a new direction. The usual hustle and bustle of the city below felt miles away as the kids gathered around, their faces curious about what was coming next. "We're going to do something different today," I announced. "I want each of you to share your dreams with us. Tell us what you want to be, using English. Don't worry about making mistakes. This is about sharing a part of you."

The kids exchanged nervous glances, but the air was charged with a sense of anticipation. Amar, always eager, volunteered to go first. Standing up, he cleared his throat, a little nervous but mostly excited. "I want to work in another country," he started, his voice gaining confidence as he spoke. "I want to speak English with people from all over the world." He paused, looking around at his friends. "It's about seeing new places, meeting new people. And I want to make my dad proud, show him there's a whole world out there."

His words were simple but filled with a deep longing for something beyond our little rooftop classroom. It was a moment that made us all pause and reflect on the power of dreams and ambition.

Next was Sohan's turn. He stood up, shy at first but then found his voice. "I dream of being a writer," he said softly. "I have stories inside me that I want to share with everyone." There was a raw honesty in his voice that touched us all.

His declaration was met with a moment of quiet respect from the group. Then, lightening the mood, one of the kids quipped, "Hope your stories are clearer than your English assignments, Sohan!" The laughter that followed was warm and encouraging, a reminder of the camaraderie we shared.

This exercise, meant to be a simple English-speaking practice, turned into a heartfelt sharing of hopes and dreams. As the sun set, painting the sky with brilliant hues of orange and pink, our rooftop felt like a small oasis of dreams in the vast city.

Each child's turn to speak was a revelation, a window into their hopes for the future. And as they spoke, it wasn't just their English that improved; it was their confidence, their belief in themselves, and their ability to dream big.

After the last student had shared, the kids began to pack up, their chatter filling the air with energy. But the impact of what we'd shared lingered, a reminder of why we were all here.

I stayed back, looking over the empty rooftop that had just been alive with the voices of the future – writers, travellers, dreamers. The quiet that followed starkly contrasted the lively session we'd just had. It gave me a moment to reflect on the importance of what we were doing here, beyond just learning a language. We were learning to dream in it too.

After our lesson about dreams, as everyone was leaving, Sohan came up to me, a bit shy. In his hand, he held some papers. "I wrote some stories," he said quietly, almost like he was unsure about it. "Can you read them?" He handed me the papers and left quickly, not waiting for my answer.

I looked at the papers in my hand and then at Sohan walking away. It felt special that he trusted me with his stories. I found a spot on the rooftop where I usually sit and started to smooth out the papers. The city was getting noisy as the evening started, but up here, it was still peaceful.

Sohan's handwriting was all over the place, but that didn't matter. I began to read, and with each word, I felt like I was seeing a bit of Sohan's world. His stories were about things he saw and imagined, some about friends, some about adventures, and some just about looking at the world and wondering about it.

As I read, I realised how much Sohan noticed things, even things that most people don't talk about. His stories made me smile because they were so honest and full of what he felt and thought.

I was really into reading when I noticed it was getting dark. The stories Sohan wrote were more than just homework or an assignment; they were a bit of him, his way of sharing how he sees things.

I knew I had to tell him the next day how much I liked his stories, and how he should keep writing. It felt important to encourage him, to let him know that what he has to say matters. His story is

The Plastic

Once there was a boy, his name Arjun. He lives near the big, big sea. He loves the sea very much. Every day after school, he runs to the sea to watch water and the fishes.

One sunny day, Arjun sees something very special. It was a turtle, but not just any turtle. This turtle was big and looked very beautiful but also very sad. Why? Because it was caught in plastic. Arjun felt very sad to see a turtle like this. He decided he must do something. So, he carefully took the plastic from the turtle. The turtle looks at Arjun, and Arjun thinks it says thank you with its eyes. From that day, Arjun and turtle, he calls her Moana, become best friends.

But Arjun also sees too much plastic in the sea. This is very bad for sea animals. He wants to help. He thinks and thinks. Then he had an idea.

Arjun goes to talk to his friends in the village. He tells them about Moana and how the sea is in danger because of plastic. At first, friends do not really understand why Arjun worries so much. But Arjun did not give up. He shows them how beautiful the sea is and how plastic harms it.

They all start to clean the beach every week. This hard work but they start to see change. Many people join them, even from other places. They all work together to make the sea safe for animals like Moana.

One amazing day, while they were cleaning the beach, they found many baby turtles, like Moana, going to sea. They feel very happy. They know they are helping.

Arjun learns that even one person can make a big difference. If all work together, they can make even bigger changes. He promised to always protect the sea and animals in it. Moana, a big beautiful turtle, is always there, watching over Arjun and his friends helping the sea.

This story of Arjun and Moana becomes famous in the village. It teaches everyone that the sea is important and we need to take care of it. Arjun is known as friend of sea. He is very proud of this. Every time he looks at the sea, he remembers when he first met Moana. It reminds him of the friendship and journey they have together, how they help the sea together.

– Sohan

As I finished reading, I realized that this wasn't just Sohan's assignment; it was his heart speaking to mine. It made me even more determined to support and nurture these young minds, to help them express themselves, and to guide them in understanding the world's complexities through their innocent eyes.

Sohan's story, with all its imperfections, was perfect in what it aimed to achieve. It left me inspired, hopeful, and ready to continue our journey on the rooftop, one story, one lesson, one dream at a time.

A Desk Job

Just as I was beginning to truly accept the joy and fulfilment of teaching the kids, of seeing their worlds expand through words and stories, life threw me a curveball. The phone rang, cutting through the quiet aftermath of another successful day on the rooftop. It was a call I had been waiting for, yet now, its timing felt almost ironic.

The voice on the other end was clear and professional. "Your application with our company has been successful. We'd like to welcome you to our team." My heart should have leaped at the news. After all, this job represented security, a steady income, something my family desperately needed given Dad's ongoing health issues and the mounting expenses. The corporate world, with its promises of a better income, was beckoning me to put on the proverbial corporate sleeve and step into a role that society deemed respectable and secure.

Yet, as I listened to the details - the start date, the expectations, the salary - a part of me felt tethered to the rooftop, to the laughter and learning that unfolded there every evening. It was a stark contrast to the corporate environment I was about to enter. Here, in my improvised classroom under the sky, I had found something that resonated deeply with my soul. Teaching had become more than just a way to earn; it had become a way to make a difference, to connect, to grow.

I hung up the phone, the news of my job confirmation heavy in my mind. The decision should have been straightforward. The job offered a way out of financial instability, a chance to provide for my family in ways I currently couldn't. Yet, the thought of leaving behind the simple yet profound joy of teaching, of missing out on the daily discoveries and the bonds formed on that rooftop, left me feeling torn.

As I stood there, contemplating my next steps, I couldn't help but think about what Mr. Perfect would say. He had always encouraged me to follow my heart, to find purpose and fulfilment in what I do. And here I was, at a crossroads, trying to decide between the security offered by the corporate world and the fulfilment I found in teaching.

The choice was difficult, more so because it wasn't just about me. It was about my family's needs, about Dad's health, about the future. And yet, as I looked out over the rooftop, now quiet and bathed in the soft glow of the setting sun, I knew that whatever decision I made, I had to find a way to keep the essence of what I'd discovered here alive. Whether in the corporate world or on this rooftop, I needed to remember the lessons learned, the joy shared, and the difference one person can make.

Sitting here in the quiet of night,
Can't sleep, thoughts too tight.
Got a job, should feel alright,
But my heart's heavy, not light.

On my rooftop, under the sky,
Teaching kids, time just flies.
Laughter, learning, no goodbyes,
Why leave this joy behind?

Big company, steady pay,
Help my family, in a way.
But will that work make my day?
Or take my true joy away?

These kids, their dreams, their trust,
In my hands, a responsibility thrust.
Teaching them, for me, a must,
In their futures, I invest.

Money's tight, Dad's not well,
Bills pile up, life's a hard sell.
This job, a solution, easy to tell,
But in my heart, doubts swell.

Rooftop lessons, under setting sun,
Where my heart feels light, teaching's fun.
Is leaving this behind the wise run?
Or have I just begun?

Will this new path lead me astray?
Or show me life in a different way?
Can I find a middle ground to stay?
Where I can work but also play?

Writing this, my hobby, my release,
Hoping it brings my heart some peace.
This decision, a giant beast,
Praying for clarity, at least.

My passion, teaching, clear as day,
But life's demands, I cannot sway.
In this poetry, my hopes lay,
To find a path, come what may.

In simple words, my feelings spill,
This choice ahead, a bitter pill.
Yet in these lines, my spirit's will,
To find my way, a path uphill.

My heart's torn, in two, it seems,
Between my dreams and practical schemes.
In this quiet night, I dare to dream,
For a life where I can both beams.

In these verses, my soul's bare,
Reflecting on all that I care about.
A teacher, a worker, can I pair?
Is there a way to repair it?

The night grows deep, my pen still flows,
Where this journey ends, nobody knows.
But in this poem, my true heart shows,
On this path, whatever I chose.

So here I sit, in the night's embrace,
Contemplating my life's pace.
In this poetry, I find my space,
To be myself, in any case.

Mr. Perfect always said, "Do what feels right, follow what makes you happy, but never forget the impact your choices have on those you care about."

Chapter 9:
The Desk Job Dilemma

The alarm went off loud at 6:00 AM, and the sound pulled me right out of sleep. Today wasn't just any normal day. It was my first day at a new job that felt a whole lot different from anything I'd done before.

I got up quickly, picked out something nice to wear—a plain blouse and trousers, hoping they were right for a big company office. Stepping outside, I saw the usual morning rush in my neighbourhood. Kids lugging big backpacks to school, laughing and yelling to each other. Some adults were hurrying along too, catching buses or out for a quick morning walk.

I walked to the bus stop where the company bus would pick me up. Standing there, waiting, I felt a mix of nervous and hopeful. This job could really help my family. It could mean we'd have more money and wouldn't have to worry so much.

The big office bus pulled up after a few minutes. It had the company's logo on the side. Inside, a few folks glanced my way as I got on. They were probably used to seeing each other, and here I was, someone new. I found a seat by the window, settled down, and pulled out my phone to give Mom a quick call.

"I'm on my way, Mom. It's my first day," I told her, trying to sound more confident than I felt.

"That's great, dear. We're all so happy for you," Mom replied. "This job is going to be good for you. Everyone at home is excited. Just do your best!"

After hanging up, I rested my head against the window, watching the streets and shops pass by as the bus drove towards the big office building. I felt a mix of things—happy because my family was counting on me and a bit sad because I missed teaching and being outdoors with my students.

As the bus pulled into the big parking area of the office, I took a deep breath. I was ready to start this new chapter, even if it was scary. I wanted to make everyone proud and, more than anything, I wanted to make sure we were okay at home.

Stepping into the corporate world was a big step, but I was ready to give it my all, keeping my head up and hoping for the best. As I walked into the large, shiny building, I promised myself I'd try to find the good in this new job, hoping it really would help us all have a better future.

A New Start

After my first full day at the new office, the ride back home gave me a moment to reflect. It was a lot quieter than the morning rush, and I appreciated the calm to gather my thoughts.

Reaching home, I headed straight to my room, feeling the need to jot down everything about the day while it was still fresh. I pulled out my journal, a bit worn around the edges, and grabbed a pen. It's not really a formal diary; more like a place where I scribble my thoughts and feelings, sometimes messy, sometimes clear, just like how I feel most days.

Sitting on my bed, I opened to a blank page and started writing:

"Met new people at work today. Nice folks. They showed me what I'll be doing. Lots to learn but seems interesting. They say it'll be a great journey. Hope they're right. Feels like I might fit in okay."

I paused, thinking about the day—the smiles, the busy hallways, the stacks of paperwork already piling up. It was different from teaching, more structured, more confined, but the people seemed genuinely supportive.

"I think the workflow will be okay," I continued writing. *"Everyone's friendly, helpful. Made me feel welcome. Big change from the rooftop classes but could be good. Must try to balance everything."*

Then my thoughts drifted to the kids I taught each evening. The idea of not seeing them or missing out on our lessons together made me anxious. They were more than just students; they were a part of my day that I cherished.

"Hope I can still meet the kids every day. At least an hour. Need to make that work. They count on me. And I need it too, more than I thought."

As I scribbled down these thoughts, the words weren't just a record; they were a promise I was making to myself. Balancing this new corporate job with my passion for teaching wasn't going to be easy, but it was something I had to manage.

I finished writing, closed my journal, and sat there for a few more minutes. The house was quiet, the noise of the day settling down. I felt a mixture of exhaustion and determination. With that, I put away my journal and got ready for bed, hoping for the strength and wisdom to handle the dual aspects of my life. Tomorrow was another day, and I needed to be ready for it.

As the days turned into weeks, the rhythm of my new corporate life began to take over. The job that had once seemed like a new adventure was quickly becoming a demanding routine. With each passing day, the workload increased, deadlines became tighter, and the office hours stretched longer than I had anticipated. This intense pace started to impact my teaching schedule, something I had promised myself to maintain.

Initially, I managed to juggle both commitments, running from the office to the rooftop for daily classes with the kids. But slowly, as the demands of the job grew, I found myself having to cut down on our sessions. My daily classes with the kids started to become less frequent. What used to be every day turned into every other day, then just twice a week, and finally, down to once a week. Each time I had to cut back on our classes, it felt like I was losing a little bit of something important.

Even though my new job at the office was really busy and took up a lot of my time, it was helping us a lot at home. The money I was earning was enough to take care of Dad's medical bills, which was a huge relief for everyone. It felt good to know that because of this job, we didn't have to worry so much about money and could pay for the care Dad needed.

But even with this good feeling about helping my family, I really missed my time teaching the kids. Teaching them wasn't just a job for me; it was something I loved to do, something that was a big part of who I am. Now, most of my time was spent in the office, and even though it was good for my family, it was hard for me because my heart was still with the kids on the terrace.

Balancing these two parts of my life was really tough. The office job brought stability and helped us with Dad's health costs, but teaching gave me joy and kept me connected to what I truly loved. As I got busier at work, I kept thinking about the kids and our classes, hoping that I wouldn't have to give them up completely.

The job slowly started to consume all my time and energy. Day by day, I found myself drifting away from everything else that mattered to me. It was not just the teaching that I was missing out on, but also the chance to connect with others around me. At work, I often felt isolated. It wasn't that my colleagues weren't kind—they were—but I just couldn't find the way to fit in.

Spending the whole day in a place where I felt I couldn't really connect with anyone was tough. It's not that I was judging the people there; it's just that I found myself in a lonely space. I wasn't in the right headspace to make friends or be a part of a circle. This sense of isolation grew each day, making the office feel even more distant and impersonal.

One day, I saw a colleague, Pragathi, celebrating her birthday. It was a big celebration right there in the office, with everyone gathered around her, laughing and sharing good wishes. The gifts she received were impressive and clearly expensive. Watching this, I couldn't help but feel a pang of something—was it envy or just a deep sense of longing? It wasn't about wanting what Pragathi had in terms of material things. It was about wanting to feel connected, to feel a part of something.

Seeing her surrounded by friends and celebration made me think about my own situation. I was there too, in the same office, but it felt like I was on the outside looking in. I started to wonder, why don't I deserve this kind of happiness? Why can't I have friends to collaborate with or just go out for a fun evening? There was this growing feeling of inferiority inside me, a whisper telling me maybe I wasn't cool enough for them, or maybe my background of constant struggle and hardship set me apart too much.

My life had always been a series of challenges—fighting through poverty, making sacrifices, and pushing through pain. And here, in this new environment, those old feelings of not being enough, of not fitting in, started to resurface. It made me question my place there, whether I would ever find my footing in a world that seemed so alien to the life I had known.

One day at work, I ended up staying much later than usual. Usually, the office starts emptying out well before I leave, but that day, everyone was gone and it was just me and Jay from marketing still at our desks. As I finally shut down my computer and began to pack up, I noticed Jay was also just about finished.

He caught me looking his way and said, *"It's really late, did work keep you back?"*

"Yeah, just one of those days where the work doesn't stop coming," I replied, slinging my bag over my shoulder.

"Seems like you're often here late too?" I asked him, curious if this was a regular thing for him.

"Yeah, I find it easier to work when it's quieter," he explained, smiling. *"No rush, I guess."*

We left the building together. When we got outside, I realised I had missed the last bus that stops near the office, which meant I had to head to the main road to catch a different one. I mentioned this to Jay, preparing myself for a long walk alone.

"Oh, I'm heading that way too. I'll walk with you if you don't mind," Jay offered.

At first, I hesitated, not wanting to inconvenience him, but he seemed genuinely fine with it, so we started walking together. The streets were less crowded now, much quieter than during the day. It was nice to have some company, especially since the walk was longer and a bit lonelier than I preferred.

As we walked down the quiet evening streets, he glanced over and asked, *"So, how are you finding the job so far?"*

"It's okay, I guess. A big change from what I'm used to," I responded, adjusting my bag on my shoulder.

"What did you do before this?" he inquired, genuinely interested.

"I was teaching kids, up on my building's terrace. Just local kids from around my neighbourhood. We'd meet after school, and I'd help them with their English or whatever they were studying," I shared, my voice growing warmer as I spoke of my past routine.

"That sounds pretty amazing. Why'd you stop?" he asked, looking over with a curious expression.

I sighed, *"It's a long story. But a big part of it was needing a stable job, something that could help with my family's needs... medical bills, you know."*

Jay nodded, *"Makes sense. But it sounds like you really loved it."*

I smiled, half-heartedly, *"I did. And I still get to teach a little, but it's not the same. There's this guy, Mr. Perfect, who really inspired me to teach. He believed in making a difference through education."*

"Mr. Perfect?" Jay chuckled softly. *"That's an interesting name."*

I laughed a bit, *"Yeah, it's what everyone calls him. He's my grandfather. He was always there, supporting my dreams, pushing me to do what I love. He was perfect in my eyes, hence the name."*

"That's really special. It sounds like he made a big impact on your life," Jay said, his tone respectful.

"Absolutely, he shaped who I am in many ways. Sometimes I wonder if I should have just stuck with teaching full-time. I miss it a lot."

As we continued walking, Jay seemed thoughtful. After a moment, he said, *"You know, I have friends who work at an NGO. They do a lot of educational programs for underprivileged kids. It sounds like something you'd be really great at."*

That caught my attention, *"Really? That does sound like something I'd love. Teaching, but also making a broader impact."*

"Yeah, I think so too. It might be worth exploring if you ever decide to go back to that kind of work," he suggested kindly.

For the first time in a long while, I felt like someone understood what I was going through. Here was someone who wasn't just hearing my words but was actually listening to what was behind them. It felt freeing to talk about my passion for teaching and how much I missed it without feeling judged for not being satisfied with my current job.

As we approached the bus stop, I felt lighter than I had in weeks. It was refreshing to talk so openly about my dreams and concerns. Jay's insight and his suggestion about the NGO gave me something to think about, a possible path that could align more with what I truly wanted to do.

After we said our goodbyes and he headed off in his direction, I continued walking home. It was getting darker, and the street lamps cast long shadows on the sidewalk. As I neared my house, I noticed a familiar figure waiting near the front steps. It was Sohan, one of my students from the terrace classes.

His eyes lit up when he saw me, and he came over and gave me a big hug. *"I've missed the classes so much,"* he said, his voice soft and sincere. *"I even stopped writing. It just doesn't feel right without your guidance."*

Hearing him say this really hit home. Sohan was always so keen during our lessons, always the first to try writing his own stories. It saddened me to hear he'd stopped, all because our classes weren't happening as often.

"We're just stuck, you know? Right where you left us," he continued, looking up at me with those hopeful eyes. *"But I came here to see if you're okay."*

It warmed my heart to know he cared that much. Despite his own struggles with not writing and missing the classes, he was here to check on me. We stood there for a bit, just talking outside my house under the dim light of the street lamps.

"That means a lot, Sohan," I said, trying to keep my voice steady. *"I promise, I'm going to try and find*

a way to hold our classes more often. You guys are really important to me."

He smiled then, a small, shy smile. *"I just want to keep writing. Your stories made me feel like I could do that too."*

We chatted a bit more about his ideas for new stories and how things were going at home. Eventually, it was time for him to go, but that conversation stayed with me long after he left.

That night, I sat up thinking for a long time. The house was quiet, and I was alone with my thoughts. Sohan's visit made me realise how much I missed teaching and how important it was for me to get back to it. Yes, my new job was helping us financially, especially with Dad's medical bills, but teaching was where my heart was.

I knew I had to find a way to do both. It wouldn't be easy, but seeing Sohan and hearing how much he missed the classes gave me the push I needed. I had to balance my job and my passion for teaching, not just for me, but for my kids on the terrace too.

The alarm blared at 6:00 AM, ripping me from the little sleep I had managed. Today wasn't just another day—it was becoming harder to get up, harder to gear up for the job that I once thought would change everything.

I got dressed quickly, choosing the same plain blouse and trousers I wore on better days. They used to make me feel prepared; now they just felt routine. As I stepped outside, the neighbourhood was waking up. Kids with heavy backpacks were half-running to school, their laughter filling the morning air. Nearby, adults hurried to catch their buses, everyone wrapped up in their daily rush.

I walked to the bus stop, feeling the weight of the day already. This job, meant to be a lifeline for my family, was now a chain. I needed it, but every day felt longer, every morning harder.

When the company bus arrived, I climbed on. The familiar faces of colleagues greeted me with nods. They all seemed to belong here more than I did. I found a seat by the window, the cool glass reminding me of how detached I felt.

As the bus started moving, I tried to lose myself in the passing scenery, but my thoughts wouldn't quiet. Then, my phone began to ring.

It was a call from home...

Chapter 10:
Heartbreak and Loss

"Mamali, your Ma is no more," Dad said. His words felt distant as if they came from far away, and nothing he said after that made it through to me.

I was sitting there, frozen, my phone slipping a bit in my hand. All I could hear was silence, drowning out the sounds of people talking around me. I kept seeing glimpses of Mom - her warm smile, how she sang while cooking, her gentle hands tucking me in at night. Her voice, always calm and soothing, now just echoes in my head.

A heavy numbness took over me, my heart feeling empty like something important was missing. I couldn't figure out why I couldn't cry. Why did I feel so hollow inside?

Ma was always the heart of our home. Even on the hardest days, she made sure we had enough to eat. She'd serve everyone first, and often, she'd end up with the smallest portion herself. But she never complained. She gave everything with love, and never once did she put herself first.

Now, with her gone, it felt like a part of me had vanished too. I remembered her lullabies, the way her voice could soothe any fear. How could I continue knowing I'd never hear her sing again,

I kept asking myself, "Ma, why can't I cry for you?" The pain was there, a deep, aching void where her love had once filled me up. I felt lost, disconnected from the world that kept moving outside the bus window. Inside, everything had stopped; time had paused, leaving me behind with my silent grief.

Why, Ma? Why?

All I could think about was getting home to Dad and Gyan. They needed me now. I found myself on another bus. She was more than just my mother; she was a pillar of strength and kindness, her heart so large it seemed to envelop everyone she met. She lived to make others happy, always placing their needs before her own. And she was always so proud of me—her support unwavering, her love boundless.

Looking out the window, watching the scenery rush by, I thought about something Mr. Perfect once said: "The best thing the universe can give you is a mother." It really hit home. Now that she's no longer here, I feel a deep emptiness, missing her so much. It's funny how we always assume there will be more time. More time to chat, to have a good laugh, to just be together with our loved ones. And then, in a blink, time runs out.

I regretted not spending more time with her, not telling her more often how much she meant to me. Those lost moments now haunted me, a reminder of what I had taken for granted. I wished for just one more day, one more conversation. But instead, I was returning to a home that would never be the same, to a family that needed me to be strong.

I remember one day when I came back from school feeling really upset. Some kids at school had been mean, making fun of my skin color and our family's lack of money. I was so angry and hurt, wondering why I had to go through all this. When Ma saw me walk in, her face filled with concern.

"What happened, Mamali?" she asked gently.

I couldn't speak. The words were stuck in my throat, choked by my tears. After a moment, I blurted out a question that had been burning inside me. *"Why was I even born?"*

Ma's face changed immediately. Tears welled up in her eyes. It pained her to hear her child say something so hurtful about herself. She didn't say anything; she just walked away. I didn't understand then why she left the room so suddenly, leaving me alone with my heavy thoughts.

After a while, I noticed she wasn't anywhere in the house. Panic set in as I called out for her with no reply. I ran outside, searching everywhere. The evening had turned the sky dark, and a cold breeze was picking up. I checked near the fields and then near the lake where she sometimes went to sit and think.

There she was, sitting quietly by the water's edge. The sight of her brought a mix of relief and more confusion. Why was she sitting all alone in the dark? Sand whipped around by the breeze stung my eyes as I ran toward her, making me blind for a moment. The darkness when I closed my eyes felt scarier than the night around me.

Ma heard me stumbling and came over quickly. She gently blew the sand from my eyes and held me close. *"Why did you leave?"* I asked.

She hugged me tighter and then looked into my eyes. *"You are the happiness we always wanted,"* she said. *"You are the reward for our struggles. I would bring the world down for you to play. Your smile makes us forget all our worries and the poverty that shadows us. You are the wish we wished for."*

I felt her tears drop onto my shoulder as she spoke. *"Your laughter, it's like medicine. It heals us, makes us forget our struggles, even if just for a moment."*

I buried my face deeper into her shoulder, still confused, still hurting. *"But why did you leave earlier? I was scared, Ma."*

She stroked my hair gently, her presence soothing me. *"My Mamali, I'll always be here for you,"* she assured me. *"When you feel lost or miss me, just find a mirror. Look closely. You'll see parts of me in you."*

As I opened the door, the sound of many voices filled the house. It was crowded with neighbours and relatives who had come to show their care. Gyan was in the middle of it all, trying his best to manage things alone.

When he saw me, he quickly came over and hugged me tightly. He started crying hard, and his tears showed just how much he was hurting. I held him, feeling his pain mix with mine.

Dad was sitting quietly, looking very weak and deeply sad. It was clear he had no strength left, not even to grasp this new reality of losing her.

I held Gyan close, trying to give him some strength, but inside, I felt completely empty. No tears came, only a deep, hollow feeling. All around, people were crying and showing their sadness openly, while I felt stuck, unable to let my own tears flow.

As the day turned into night and people began to leave, the house grew very quiet. The silence was loud, reminding us of what we had lost.

We started to prepare for the cremation, following all the traditional steps our family has always followed. Each action was a way to honour Ma's life. We wrapped her in her favourite sari, setting up everything as our traditions teach us.

Gyan lit the lamp and placed flowers around Ma. The smell of flowers and incense filled the air, sweet but sad.

During these rituals, I felt like I was just going through the motions. Gyan, however, was fully involved, his grief clear in every action and prayer.

Sitting next to Ma later, I looked at her peaceful face and remembered all the times we shared. *"Why can't I cry, Ma? Why do I feel so empty instead of sad?"*

After Gyan left the house, he didn't come back for a long time. He was struggling to handle everything, and I understood that. Dad, on the other hand, was completely shattered. He had lost the person who had been his strength for so many years. I wanted to comfort him, but he seemed too far gone in his grief, unreachable in his sorrow.

Unable to stay inside with all the weight of our collective pain, I found myself walking aimlessly. The cool night air was a small relief from the stuffiness of the house crowded with sadness. Without realising it, my feet led me to the lake—a place Ma often visited to find peace.

It was dark, and the first hints of dawn were just starting to light the sky. As I stood there, lost in my thoughts, it almost felt as if Ma was there with me. In my heart, I could see her sitting beside the lake, just as she often did, looking serene and thoughtful. For a moment, it was as if she was there, one more time, just us together.

I blinked, and for a second, it seemed like my eyes met hers. She was smiling at me, that warm, reassuring smile that had always made everything better. The vision was so real, that for a heartbeat, I believed it.

"Ma," I whispered into the quiet, my voice breaking the silence around the lake

As I stared into the lake, my reflection on the water seemed like a mirror image of myself, blurring slightly with the gentle ripples. Suddenly, I remembered what Ma once told me, her words echoing clearly in my mind: **"If you miss me, look in the mirror, I'm in you."** Those words hit me harder than ever before, breaking the dam I hadn't realised was holding back my emotions.

At that moment, the tears I had been unable to shed began to flow freely. The sobs came from deep within, loud and heart-wrenching, as I mourned not just her death but the physical absence of the person who had been my world. *"I miss you, Ma,"* I cried out, my voice carrying over the still water. *"You will always be a part of me."*

She gave me life, not just by bringing me into this world, but by showing me how to truly live. Her teachings on love, resilience, and kindness formed the basis of my existence. Now, without her physical presence, it feels like I'm navigating life all over again. As tears fell next to the lake, I sensed her spirit surrounding me. It felt like she was there, letting me know she's still looking out for me. This assurance brought me a mix of comfort and sadness. Though she's gone, her legacy lives on through me. The strength she shared through years of loving guidance is now mine to carry forward.

"I will continue your legacy of love, Ma," I said through tears. *"I promise to live in a way that honours you."*

In the quiet morning light, I write,
Words for you, Ma, who taught me to fight.
Not with fists, but with love and grace,
In every challenge, I seek your face.

You are the whisper of the wind through the trees,
The warmth of the sun, the calm in the breeze.
In every heartbeat, in each breath I take,
Your strength and love, they help me make.

I write for you, the lullabies you sang,
Your laughter in my ears, the joy you rang.
You gave without asking, loved without bounds,
In my heart, Ma, your spirit resounds.

This is for you, the life you've sown,
In your love, a garden beautifully grown.
Though now you're gone, you're here with me,
In every mirror, your face I see.

You taught me life, not just to exist,
To love, to dream, to persist.
Your legacy, Ma, forever will last,
In my actions, my future, my past.

Chapter 11:
A Renewed Mission

As the days went by, the emptiness left by Ma's absence seemed to grow larger. Dad's health was failing, and he needed constant care. I was there, trying to fill the void, but I knew I could never replace her. The house felt different, quieter, as if it too missed her presence. Gyan was hardly ever home now; his absence added to the loneliness that seemed to hang in every corner.

One morning, as I helped Dad with his medicine, I couldn't shake the feeling of being utterly overwhelmed. It wasn't just about the physical tasks of caring for him; it was the emotional weight of seeing him so fragile, so unlike the strong father he had always been. Everything at home reminded me of her, from the way the sunlight fell across the kitchen floor where she used to stand, to the chair she favored in the living room, now empty.

I missed her terribly. The house did too. And Gyan... I hadn't seen him in days. Where was he? Why had he distanced himself so much? It felt like I was losing my family bit by bit, not just to death but to the spaces between us that kept growing.

This feeling of disconnection made me think back to a time when it was all different, when we were all together, united by her presence.

Sitting next to Dad, listening to his slow breaths, I drifted into a memory from a long summer day years ago. Mr. Perfect and I were sitting under the big neem tree by our house. I was upset about something that felt huge at the time, but really wasn't.

"Life's a lot like this old tree, Mamali," he said, touching the rough bark. "It keeps growing, no matter how tough the weather is. It doesn't stop because it's hard; it keeps reaching up because it has a reason to."

I looked up at him. The sunlight came down through the leaves, making patterns on his face. "What if it gets too hard?" I asked.

He laughed softly, his eyes all wrinkled up. "Then it gets hard. But that doesn't mean you stop walking your path. Every step you take, even if it's tough, is worth it because it leads you somewhere important."

His words were comforting, like they always were. "You've got a long way to go, my dear. And it's worth all the effort. You're meant to teach, to help others, to make a difference. Remember that."

Thinking about those days teaching on the rooftop brought a smile to my face, even though things were tough now. I missed being there with my students, seeing their eager faces each day. That work felt right, like I was really doing something good.

Just as I was lost in these memories, *my phone rang.*

As I held the phone, my team leader's voice came through with a mix of concern and formality.

"Hello, Mamali. How are you holding up? We've all heard about your loss, and we're deeply sorry," she began, her voice gentle.

"Thank you," I replied, the words heavy in my throat. *"It's been very hard."*

There was a brief pause before she continued, *"We understand this is a difficult time for you, but we need to talk about work. It's been quite some time, and we need to plan for the team's tasks. Do you know when you might return?"*

Her question made me pause. My family needed me, yet work was calling me back.

"I'm not sure yet," I admitted, feeling a bit lost. "Things are still uncertain here, but I understand the team's needs. Can I have a few days to figure things out?"

"Of course, take the time you need. Just keep us informed, please. Your role is important to us, and we look forward to your return when you're ready," she responded, her voice warm but professional.

"Thank you for your understanding. I'll keep you updated," I assured her, hanging up with mixed feelings.

Sitting quietly, I reflected on her words. They reminded me of Mr. Perfect's advice about moving forward. Life doesn't wait; it pushes us to continue, even when it's hard.

"I can't just stop," I told to myself, feeling a resolve build inside. "Ma would want me to keep going, to use her teachings to make something good happen."

I went to Dad, knowing it was time to talk about going back to work. I found him in his usual place by the window, looking out but not really seeing anything. I sat down next to him, taking his hand in mine.

"Dad, I think I need to go back to work. They called today."

He turned to look at me, his eyes tired but understanding. *"I know, beta,"* he said gently. *"You have responsibilities. You need to go back."*

"But what about you? And Gyan?" I asked, the worry clear in my voice.

He held my hand, giving me a small, reassuring smile. *"I'll manage here. Don't worry about me. It's not easy, but I understand. Your place isn't just here with me. You have your own path to walk."*

His words were simple but they carried a weight, a permission and a blessing wrapped in one. *"Go on, beta. Do what you need to do. Make your way. I'm always here, and I'm proud of you, no matter where you are."*

Leaving the room, I felt a mix of relief and sorrow. Dad's words had given me the push I needed, but they also reminded me of the heavy choice I had to make. Balancing family and career, presence and absence—it wasn't going to be easy. But as I packed my bag that night, I knew it was the right thing to do. For them, for me. Life had to move forward, and so did I.

I went to look for Gyan, feeling worried about what was ahead. I found him sitting quietly by the river, our favourite place to talk and think.

I sat next to him, leaving some space between us. *"Gyan,"* I said calmly, *"I need to go back to work. We need the money, and Dad needs care I can't give on my own."*

He didn't say anything at all, just kept looking at the water. It wasn't like him to be so quiet.

"Gyan, please talk to me," I asked gently. *"Will you be okay handling things with Dad?"*

But he stayed quiet, his shoulders tight, his eyes fixed on the water.

"Gyan, please, say something."

Still, he didn't move or speak. His silence felt like a wall, blocking me out when I needed to connect with him the most.

I put my hand on his shoulder, trying to show him how important this was. *"We need to support each other,"* I said gently. *"I'll come back whenever I can, and you can call me, anytime."*

He didn't react to my touch or my words. His silence was a gap growing wider between us.

As I got up to leave, feeling the weight of our new reality, I added, *"Look after Dad. And yourself. Remember, you're stronger than you think."*

Walking away, his silence stayed with me, heavy with everything unspoken as I left him by the river, the cool evening air filling the space between us.

It is me, Gyan

I was standing there, not moving, watching Mamali get ready to leave. Suddenly, a memory came to me, clear and strong.

I was just a little kid back then. Ma and Dad had gone to help Mr. Perfect because he was sick. They left Mamali and me at home. I didn't really get why they had to go. The house felt too quiet, and I started to feel scared.

I hid under the table, trying to disappear. The fear was huge; it filled up the room. Then I heard footsteps and saw Mamali bending down to look under the table. When she saw me, she smiled.

"It's okay, I'm here," she told me gently. "We'll be fine until Mom and Dad come home." Her voice made me feel better. She stayed with me, played with me, and told me stories until our parents came back. By the time they did, I wasn't scared anymore.

Now, as Mamali was packing up to leave, that old fear of being alone came back strong. I couldn't just let her go without telling her how much she meant to me, how she helped me that day.

I knew I had to do something. So, I turned around and ran back to the house. I needed to catch her before she left, to show her that just like she was there for me, I'd always be there for her.

I hurried as fast as I could, hoping to catch Mamali before she left. The streets were mostly empty, and I pushed myself to run faster. When I got to our house, she was already gone. I didn't stop; I ran straight to the bus stop, hoping she was still there.

And there she was, standing alone, looking distant. She turned as she heard me approaching. I slowed down, trying to steady my breathing, and managed a smile. *"Go,"* I said between breaths. *"I'll take care of Dad. You don't need to worry."*

She looked at me, maybe a bit surprised to see me there. I wanted to lighten the mood, make it easier for her. *"And hey,"* I added, trying to joke a little, *"don't forget about us when you're out there making it big."*

That got a small laugh from her, and she came over to hug me. *"Take care, okay?"* she said softly.

We let go, and she stepped back as the bus rolled up. She gave me a long look, one that said a lot without words, then she got on. I watched the bus drive away, feeling a mix of things—worry for her, relief that I could be there for Dad, and a little pride too.

Standing there, watching the bus disappear, I felt a resolve settling in. She was going to be alright. And back home, I'd make sure everything was alright too.

Chapter 12:
The Gateway Opportunity

Back at the office, each day felt longer than the last. Sitting at my desk, surrounded by piles of work, it seemed like the tasks just kept growing. From the moment I arrived in the morning until I left at night, I was drowning in a sea of paperwork, emails, and endless reports.

Every morning, I'd walk into the office hoping to make a dent in the workload, but by lunchtime, it felt like I hadn't made any progress. The office was always buzzing—phones ringing, keyboards clicking, and coworkers chatting. It was overwhelming, and I felt lost in the shuffle.

Lunch breaks were short and hardly a break at all. I'd sit and try to relax, but my mind was always on the tasks waiting for me. It was like a brief pause in a long marathon, just enough to catch my breath before diving back in.

As the day wore on and the office began to empty, I often found myself still there, working in the quiet. The glow from my computer screen was my only company as I tried to finish just one more thing before heading home.

Walking home after such exhausting days, I'd reflect on everything I'd done, but it never felt like enough.

The next morning would just bring more of the same: more tasks, more pressure, more sitting at that desk feeling disconnected from it all.

Lately, my job feels like a never-ending cycle. Each day, I arrive at the office and face a desk buried under so much work that it's hard to see an end to it. I've been trying to catch up ever since I returned, working non-stop, barely noticing the hours ticking by.

One evening, just when I thought I was finally getting somewhere with the workload, I made a big mistake on a report. It was the kind of mistake you don't see until someone else points it out – and that's exactly what happened.

My manager found the error and called me into his office. It felt like the walk to his office took forever. When I entered, I found him sitting there with the report in hand, looking very serious. He held up the document and pointed straight at the error.

"This can't happen again," he said, his voice firm and a bit louder than usual. His words hit me hard. I stood there, feeling my face get warm. I wanted to explain, to say how tired I had been, but the words didn't come out.

I just nodded, feeling embarrassed and small. It was tough standing there, knowing I had slipped up. All I could think about was how much I needed this job, how important the salary was for my family. It felt like I was carrying a heavy weight, one that got heavier with each passing moment in his office.

When I finally left his office, the office seemed quieter than usual, or maybe it was just me feeling more alone. I went back to my desk, my hands shaking a little as I sat down. The noise of typing and phone calls around me felt distant, like I was underwater.

I just kept thinking, *"I have to keep this job. I have to."*

Sitting alone in the canteen, I was lost in my thoughts when Jay walked over with his lunch tray and sat across from me. He looked concerned as he settled in.

"How's everything at home?" he asked, breaking the silence. I just shook my head, finding it hard to put everything into words.

"It's tough," I said simply.

Jay nodded, understanding there was more behind my words. He wanted to help, to lift my spirits, but knew some situations were too complex for quick fixes.

After a brief pause, he brought up a new topic. *"You remember the NGO I volunteer with? They're running a small program this weekend and need volunteers, especially for teaching. It might be nice for you to join."*

I hesitated. The idea of teaching again, even if just for a weekend, brought a mix of excitement and uncertainty.

"Jay, I... I'm not sure," I replied.

"Come on," he encouraged. *"It's just for a weekend, and it's something good. You miss teaching, right? This could be a good chance for you."*

Thinking it over, I felt a spark of interest. Maybe this was what I needed—a return to something familiar that could also feel new.

"Okay," I finally agreed, a small smile forming. *"Yes, I'll do it. It sounds like a good idea."*

Jay smiled brightly. *"Awesome! It's going to be great, and you'll be helping out a lot. It's really a win-win."*

As he got up to leave, I felt a hint of the old enthusiasm I used to have. Maybe this weekend program was the opportunity I needed.

"Thanks, Jay," I called after him as he walked away. *"I appreciate it."*

New Path

As the weekend arrived, I found myself walking toward the venue where the NGO program was set to happen. As I arrived, I stopped for a moment, amazed at the number of kids there. They were everywhere, all waiting for someone to teach and guide them.

Jay noticed me right away and came over with a friendly smile.

"Hey! I'm so glad you're here," he said warmly. *"Let's get you started with the other volunteers."*

We walked past groups of kids. Some were playing quietly, others chatting. The place was lively, full of young energy that reminded me of my teaching days.

"We're about to start the volunteer introduction," Jay explained as he led me to a group of volunteers. *"You'll meet everyone else and learn about what we're doing this weekend."*

While waiting for the event to begin, I overheard two young girls talking nearby. One girl, with her hair tied back, looked worried. *"Why do we even need to study more? Isn't school enough?"* she asked.

Her friend replied, *"School's just to pass time. But now they make us come here too. More studying? We could be helping at home, making some money."*

"Yeah," the first girl added, "we go to school because we have to, then we work. Now this? What's the point? It's not like we're going to become doctors or something."

I listened to their conversation, feeling both sad and understanding. Their words showed the tough choice between needing to earn money now and the potential benefits of education for their future.

Lost in thought, I barely noticed the crowd's attention shift until a familiar voice brought me back to the present. It was Mr. Vaashi, my old professor, stepping up to the center stage. He adjusted the microphone, and a hush fell over the crowd.

Seeing him there, the founder of this NGO, was a surprise that jolted me. His presence was a bridge between my past and these kids' potential futures, a symbol of education's transformative power. His first words began to address precisely the concerns I'd just overheard, but now with a gentle authority that demanded attention.

After Mr. Vaashi's speech, I walked through the crowd to say hello. He was clearly delighted to see me.

"It's wonderful to see you here!" he said, his voice full of joy.

Just as we were about to chat more, Jay tapped my shoulder, signaling that it was time to start the classes. I noticed the two young girls I overheard earlier. They seemed unsure about everything going on.

"Wait a sec, Jay," I said, and approached the girls.

"Hey, I heard you two talking earlier," I began, keeping my voice friendly. "You're wondering why you need to study more, right?"

They looked at me, surprised that I had listened in.

"Yeah, it seems like a lot," one girl replied, scuffing the dirt with her shoe.

I smiled, trying to put them at ease. "I know it feels like just more schoolwork. But what if you could learn something that lets you do new things, not just the usual stuff? Something that could make everyday tasks easier, or even fun?"

The other girl looked interested now. "Like what?"

"Think of it as if you're a superhero. Your superpower? Being really smart. You could solve problems faster, help your family in better ways, and maybe even start a business that makes you the boss," I suggested, hoping to stir their imaginations.

The first girl laughed a little. "A superhero, huh? That sounds cooler."

"Exactly!" I said, excited they were warming up to the idea. "Learning isn't just about reading books and passing tests. It's about gaining the skills you need to achieve whatever you dream of. Who knows? Maybe one day you'll be the one inspiring others or leading a big project."

The girls looked at each other, their expressions lightening up. "Okay, we'll give it a try," the second girl finally said, sounding more interested.

"Awesome! Let's see what you can learn today. And remember, it's all about discovering your superpowers," I told them, guiding them back to the class area.

As we walked, I felt a little thrill of success. Perhaps I had managed to make learning a bit more exciting for them. With that hopeful thought, I joined the other volunteers, ready to help however I could.

After the session, I felt a genuine sense of fulfillment, the kind I hadn't experienced in a long while. Mr. Vaashi watched the whole class and came over as I was getting ready to leave.

"You did really well today," he said, looking both proud and pleased. *"I'm very proud of you."*

I was about to thank him when he added, *"Have you thought about working here full time? You look truly happy when you're teaching."*

His question made me pause. *"Why do you say that?"* I asked, curious to hear his thoughts.

"Because there are many kids here who remind me of you," Mr. Vaashi explained softly. *"They need someone to guide them, inspire them. You connect with them so naturally. We need you to help them reach for more."*

I carried his words with me as I headed home. That night, as I lay in bed, Mr. Vaashi's offer kept running through my mind. Was this a new path for me? A chance to really make a difference and connect with what I loved doing?

The possibility of working in a place where I could share my passion and really affect lives felt exciting and a bit scary. As I recollect over Mr. Vaashi's words, I couldn't shake off the sense of opportunity. Maybe this was where I was meant to be, a place where I could grow and help others grow too.

The next day at the office, everything felt overwhelming. The workload was enormous, and my manager was pushing hard for deadlines. As I tried to keep up, my manager came over to my desk again.

"You need to speed up. We can't afford any delays," he insisted, looking over the stack of unfinished reports.

Each word from him added weight to the already heavy atmosphere. But then, I remembered what

Mr. Vaashi had said at the NGO: *"There are a lot of Mamalis here, they need you to go up."* His words rang in my ears, reminding me of where I felt my work truly mattered.

As I absorbed the pressure around me, I recalled a phrase Mr. Perfect often used about following what truly matters to your heart. It gave me the push I needed.

Taking a deep breath, I turned to my manager and said, *"I appreciate this opportunity, but I cannot continue. This job isn't right for me anymore.*

I'm sorry, I quit."

Chapter 13:
Should I Quit!

Back on my terrace with Amar, Sohan, and all the kids, I felt really alive again. This place, under the open sky with the kids looking up at me, was where I was meant to be, not stuck in an office.

I spent the whole day catching up with each child. Amar was proud to show me the new English words he could now spell. Sohan, a bit quieter, handed me a story he wrote. His writing was neater than before, and he looked up at me, waiting to see what I thought.

In the evening, I called Dad and Gyan to tell them about my decision. *"I've quit the job,"* I said plainly. There was a pause—Dad and Gyan were worried but they also understood.

"Are you sure about this?" Pa asked. His voice was weak but he wanted to support me.

"Yes, Pa. This makes me happy. It's where I really help," I told him, feeling sure about my choice.

Gyan didn't say much at first, then he added, *"If you're happy, then we are too. Just make sure you're also taking care of yourself."*

I promised I would. After the call, I felt so thankful for their support.

That night, looking up at stars that seemed to glow a little brighter, I thanked Mr. Perfect, my grandpa, in my thoughts. *"Thank you for teaching me that happiness comes from following your heart,"* I said softly.

Being back wasn't just about teaching again; it was about being true to myself. Here with these kids, I wasn't just their teacher—I was also learning from them about hope and joy.

As I got ready for the next day, I felt right where I was supposed to be. Leaving the office job wasn't an end; it was a new beginning, a chance to make a difference. Here on this terrace, looking out over the city with these eager kids, was exactly where I needed to be. Every day felt important and full of possibilities.

Back on my terrace, with the sky overhead,
I write down these words as new paths spread.
I've left the job, left the stress behind,
Leaving wasn't losing, it was choosing a new path,
To go back to teaching, where my heart found its laugh.
My desk is bare, my heart so light,
Here with the kids, everything feels right.
Each day we learn, together we grow,
In this place I fit, where my passions flow.
I stand here teaching, under the blue sky,
This is where I shine, where I aim to fly.
The future's unknown, but that's alright,
I'm here, content, finding my light.

What comes next, I'm not sure where or when,
But I'm ready for it, with my pen.
No map for the future, but that's okay,
I'm here, I'm happy, I'm finding my way.

Teaching on the terrace feels just right. Hearing the kids laugh and seeing them learn warms my heart. But when the noise fades and I'm alone, I start to worry. The NGO hasn't called yet. *Did I quit my steady job too soon?*

Day after day goes by. I walk down streets I've known all my life, stopping to buy food at the usual places. These are the tastes and sounds of my childhood, but now they remind me of what I might have given up.

Sitting down, watching the traffic pass, I think hard about my choices. I love teaching, but can it really support my family? As the evening comes and the streetlights turn on, I feel more unsure.

At home, it's too quiet. My phone doesn't ring, and I wonder if I've made a big mistake.

The next day started with a surprise. My phone rang, and on the other end was good news: the NGO had confirmed my job. A wave of relief washed over me, replacing the uncertainty of the past weeks. I was happy, really happy for the first time in a while.

When I arrived at the NGO the following day, the atmosphere was entirely different from my previous office job. This place is filled with a variety of people—diverse in culture, with some physically disabled individuals among them, all engaged in meaningful work. It was refreshing to see such inclusivity; here, everyone was treated equally, with dignity and respect.

As I walked through the office, observing people collaborating and sharing smiles, I felt a sense of belonging. This was a community where everyone mattered, where every voice was valued.

During the orientation, I was handed my first major task. They wanted me to prepare and present a proposal to a corporate sponsor, aiming to secure funds for an upcoming project. And I heard something that made me pause: Mr. Vaashi had specifically recommended me for this responsibility. Knowing he trusted me this much boosted my confidence.

It was a big assignment, but I felt ready. The trust Mr. Vaashi showed in me wasn't just a vote of confidence in my abilities; it was a reminder of why I had chosen this path. Here, in this environment, I could make a real difference, not just in my life but in the lives of others too.

As the day for the presentation came closer, I worked hard on every part of it. I wanted to make sure everything was clear and strong. This presentation wasn't just for me; it was for our NGO and all the good work we do.

On that day, I felt nervous. I arrived at the corporate office, which was a big and busy place, very different from our NGO office. I checked in at the front desk, holding my notes and laptop a bit tightly.

The receptionist told me to go to a meeting room upstairs. I took the elevator, trying to calm down by going over my main points.

When I got to the meeting room, someone from the company welcomed me and showed me inside. The room was big and bright, with a large table and many chairs around it. People started to come in and say hello as they sat down. I set up my laptop, hearing every click of the keyboard.

Soon, everyone was there, sitting around the table. I felt the importance of this moment. This was my chance to help our NGO. I looked around at everyone, ready to start speaking as soon as the meeting began. The room filled up, and I took a deep breath, ready to begin.

As I finished my presentation, the room's atmosphere felt indifferent. The faces around the conference table showed disinterest; it was as though they were looking right through me. I had poured my heart into every slide, every word, hoping to convey the importance of education, the impact it could have on lives like mine. But there, in those moments, it felt like speaking into a void.

The lead executive, a stern-looking man with sharp eyes, was the first to break the silence after I concluded. His words cut deeper than I expected. "This was disappointing. Why should we fund an NGO focused on education? Why should people like you even bother studying?"

His question struck a raw nerve. It wasn't just an inquiry; it was a dismissal of everything I stood for, everything I had come from. It was as if my entire journey—my struggles and triumphs—were being trivialised in front of an audience that saw no value in them.

I stood there, my confidence crumbling, feeling smaller by the second. The room felt colder, the walls seemed to draw in closer, and I felt an overwhelming urge to escape. But I stood my ground, even as my voice shook. "Education is a right, not a privilege. It's the key to breaking cycles of poverty and ignorance. It's essential for people like me, like us, to rise above our circumstances."

But the damage was done. Their minds seemed made up, and their cold glances told me nothing I said would change their views. The meeting ended abruptly, and as I walked out, their dismissive attitudes strained in my mind, taunting me. *Why shouldn't people like me study? Why shouldn't we aspire for more?*

In the cafe, Jay sat down across from me, his face showing a hint of concern. He noticed my distant look and asked, *"How's the new job treating you?"*

I didn't say much, still upset by the dismissive attitudes I'd encountered in the meeting. The indifference of those people stung deep.

Trying to lighten the mood, Jay took a napkin from the table and began folding it. *"I used to make paper rockets as a kid,"* he said as he worked the napkin into shape. "It was my way of dreaming about flying."

He finished the rocket and held it up. *"But you know, flying isn't just about launching into the sky. It's also about learning to handle the wind and knowing how to keep going once you're up there."*

I looked at the simple paper rocket in his hands. Jay wasn't just talking about paper crafts; he was giving me a metaphor for my situation. *"You need to fly,"* he said gently, *"but first, you need to learn how."*

I stood on my terrace with the paper rocket in my hand, looking out over the roofs below. The breeze was gentle, and it felt like a normal evening, but something inside me had shifted. Holding the rocket, a simple thing Jay had made from a tissue, I thought deeply. "I need to learn," I whispered to myself. "To be a good teacher, I must learn first."

Around me, the neighbourhood was quiet, with just the occasional sounds of life echoing up to where I stood. This place, my home, felt like the start of something new. The rocket, though just a bit of folded paper, seemed to symbolise hope and possibility. It made me think about starting, about trying and sometimes failing, but always learning from each attempt.

With the rocket pointing up towards the sky, I made a small promise to myself. "I will learn," I said quietly, almost as if I were making a vow. "Not just for me, but for all the kids who need someone to show them the way." This terrace, where I'd taught so many lessons and shared so many dreams with my students, felt like the right place to renew my commitment to teaching.

I knew I'd face tough rooms again, like the corporate boardroom that had shaken my confidence. Next time, I'd bring more than just presentations. I'd bring stories of what education could really do, stories that could turn doubt into support. Teaching isn't just about giving information; it's about opening minds and changing lives.

I looked at the rocket again, its tip pointing towards the sky, and smiled.

Ready for the challenges ahead, I felt a new sense of purpose. Learning, teaching, inspiring—that was my path now.

It was more than a goal; it was my way to make a real difference.

Chapter 14:
Echoes of the Past

The sun was just rising, as I prepared for a new day, a day that promised a fresh start. I had a feeling of anticipation mixed with determination. Today, I was stepping into a new role, teaching a new batch of students. I felt ready, inspired by the idea that I was about to help shape young minds.

Walking into the classroom, I was greeted by the lively chatter of kids, a sound that brought a smile to my face. *"Good morning, everyone!"* I announced, my voice bright and hopeful. The children looked up, their expressions a mixture of curiosity and excitement.

"This is going to be a fun day," I said as I arranged my teaching materials, trying to convey my enthusiasm. "We're going to learn new things, play some games, and maybe even create our own stories. Are you ready to start?"

Their nods and eager faces were the only encouragement I needed.

The room was noisy, but not with excitement. The children were restless and didn't pay much attention to the lessons I was trying to teach. I tried everything to get them interested—games, stories, asking questions— but nothing worked.

As I stood in front of them, trying again and again to grab their attention, I began to feel frustrated. My enthusiasm from the beginning of the day started to fade as each new effort to engage them failed. They whispered to each other, giggled, and seemed to pay more attention to everything else but me.

Taking a deep breath, I tried not to show how disappointed I felt. "Let's try something different," I suggested, hoping to see a spark of interest from them. But they just continued to look around, doodle in their notebooks, and seemed uninterested in what I was saying.

I felt a bit rejected standing there. This wasn't what I had pictured when I decided to come back to teaching. I thought it would be fun and full of learning, not this struggle to even get their attention.

The day ended and I felt really down. I started to question myself. *Was I not good at this anymore?* The walk home felt very long, as I thought about all the things that went wrong in class.

Day after day, I walked into the classroom with a plan to try something new, hoping to spark their interest. But it felt like hitting a wall each time. The kids remained disinterested, hardly looking up from their desks when I spoke. I tried different strategies—interactive activities, games, even incorporating music and videos into my lessons. Despite my efforts, their lack of enthusiasm was clear.

The days turned into a repetitive cycle. Each morning, I prepared with fresh hope, but by the end of the day, I felt drained and discouraged. It was tough standing there, trying to reach out to them, and not seeing any response. Their indifference weighed heavily on me, making me doubt my abilities as a teacher.

I remember standing at the front of the classroom, watching them chatter among themselves or stare blankly out the window. "Let's try to focus," I would say, attempting to bring their attention back. But they looked away quickly because they got distracted.

Feeling somewhat defeated, I'd sit at my desk after class, wondering what I could do differently. Could I break through to them somehow? The silence of the empty classroom heard back my frustrations, a reminder of the day's failures.

But I didn't want to give up. I needed to connect with these kids, get them excited about learning. It was tough, but I remembered why I was there. It wasn't just teaching; it was about making a change, even with small steps. So, I kept trying, no matter how hard it got.

One day, my patience was really tested. It was like any other frustrating day, but this time, something snapped. There was this one boy, Rahul, always the most challenging. He would throw things around, interrupt when I was talking, and make it hard for anyone to concentrate. That day, he was even more disruptive than usual, shouting and not letting me get a word in.

I tried to calm him down, asking him gently at first, then more firmly, to please settle and listen. But he just laughed and threw a crumpled paper ball right at me. Something inside me just couldn't take it anymore. Without thinking, I rushed over to him and slapped him. The slap sound filled the room, then everything went quiet. All the kids were staring.

I stood there, my hand still raised, shocked at what I had just done. I felt a mix of anger and immense guilt. I never thought I would react like that. I looked around at their stunned faces and knew I had crossed a line.

Without saying another word, I walked out of the classroom. What I had done bore down on me. I felt terrible, not just for slapping Rahul but for letting myself lose control like that. I shouldn't have slapped Rahul. That moment made me think back to my own school days, which were sometimes just as hard.

I remembered a day when my teacher told me in front of everyone that I couldn't stay in class because my fees hadn't been paid. I had to pick up my things and leave the room while everyone watched. Walking out felt so embarrassing.

The next day, I went back to school, hoping things might be different. But my teacher stopped me at the door. *"Why are you here? You know you can't come in without paying,"* she said. It felt like she wasn't just talking about the money; it was like she was saying I didn't belong there at all.

Hurt and angry, I said, *"I thought school was for learning, not just for those who can pay."* That made the other students laugh, but not the teacher. She slapped me right there, in front of everyone. It wasn't just the pain of the slap that hurt, but the shame of being hit like that in front of my classmates.

Now, back in my classroom with Rahul, I felt that old shame again. I saw his shocked face and knew I had made a big mistake. The room was quiet. All the kids were staring.

"I'm sorry, Rahul," I said softly, feeling really sorry about what I had done. "I shouldn't have slapped you. That's not the right way to handle things."

I got down to his level and looked him in the eyes. "Can we talk about what just happened? I want to understand and fix this." The classroom was still silent as we started to talk it through, trying to fix the mistake and learn from it, not just about school subjects but about how to treat each other better.

In Vaashi's room, I confessed to losing control with the kids. He listened quietly before nodding in understanding.

"I know it's tough," Vaashi said, leaning back in his chair. *"I've been there. You know, when I first started teaching, I had a class that just wouldn't warm up to me. They were just as notorious as your group."*

He chuckled a little, then continued, *"I tried everything—strict rules, lots of homework, you name it. Nothing worked. They just didn't like me. It felt like I was talking to walls every day."*

Leaning forward, Vaashi's eyes lit up a bit as he shared his breakthrough. *"Then one day, I just decided to throw out the lesson plan. I started telling them stories—silly ones, about my own school days, about the crazy things I did. I even acted out some parts, made funny faces, you know?"*

I listened, intrigued by the shift in his approach.

"And something clicked," he said with a smile. *"They started laughing, and little by little, they began to open up. They started participating, asking questions, even making jokes themselves. It was like once they saw I could laugh at myself, they felt more comfortable around me."*

He leaned in, his voice earnest. *"Humor, Mamali, can be a bridge. Once they enjoyed my jokes, everything got easier. Kids accept some people very rarely, but once they do, they surrender completely."*

I absorbed his words, thinking about how I could apply this insight. *"It sounds like you really found a way to connect with them,"*.

"Yes, and that's the key," Vaashi replied. *"Find that connection, whatever it may be. For me, it was humor. For you, it might be something else. But once you find it, hold onto it. It changes everything."*

As I left his office, I felt a bit lighter, with a new perspective. Maybe I didn't need to control every aspect of the classroom. Perhaps letting go a little and finding a way to connect on their level—through humor or shared interests—could help bridge the gap between us.

Mr Funny

One afternoon, when I was about seven, I stubbornly demanded a new toy—a colorful kite I'd seen at the market. My mom firmly told me, "No, you're not getting it just because you keep insisting." Despite her words, I threw a big tantrum right in our living room, crying loudly, hoping she'd give in.

As I cried, my mom tried to soothe me, but nothing worked. That's when Mr. Perfect arrived. Everyone else had tried and failed to calm me down.

He sat down beside me with a serious look, then suddenly smiled and said, one day, a little monkey found a banana that was stuck tight in a hole. The monkey tried to pull it out, but no matter how hard he tugged, the banana wouldn't budge. Frustrated, he started crying. An old elephant walking by saw the crying monkey and asked what was wrong.

The monkey explained, *"I can't get this banana out!"*

The elephant looked at the hole and then at the banana and said, *"I'll tell you a secret, but only if you stop crying."*

Curious, the monkey wiped his tears and nodded. The elephant leaned down and whispered, *"Maybe... the banana isn't stuck. Maybe it's just home and doesn't want to leave!"*

The monkey laughed, realizing how silly it was to assume the banana wanted to be eaten. And from that day on, whenever he found a fruit stuck in a place, he just left it there, thinking maybe it was just happy at home!

It was such a simple, silly joke, but Mr. Perfect's delivery, complete with playful gestures, made me start laughing instead of crying. As he continued with more jokes, each one sillier than the last, my tears turned into giggles.

As I laughed, I gradually forgot about the kite. Mr. Perfect gently explained, "Sometimes, a little laughter helps us see things differently. It's not always about getting what we want, but about enjoying the moment."

That day, I learned a valuable lesson about adaptability and looking at things from a new angle. Mr. Perfect's use of humor not only lifted my spirits but also shifted my perspective. It was a lesson in how sometimes, laughter can be the best way to overcome stubbornness and see past disappointments.

Recalling this, I realized I could use a similar approach with my challenging students. If humor could change my young, stubborn heart, maybe it could reach them too. Armed with this new strategy, I felt ready to transform the classroom dynamic, hoping to replace resistance with laughter and engagement.

New Joke

I walked into the classroom knowing I needed to change the mood from yesterday. The kids looked up slowly as I entered, their eyes wide and cautious. I could feel the leftover tension from yesterday, and I knew I needed to make everyone feel lighter.

"Good morning, everyone!" I said, trying to sound as cheerful as possible. I paused, giving them a moment to respond, but the room stayed quiet. Determined to shift the atmosphere, I decided to throw in some humor.

"Want to hear a joke?" I asked, and some curious looks appeared. I smiled and started with the simplest, silliest joke I knew. *"Why did the student eat his homework?"* I paused for effect, even though they were still quiet. *"Because the teacher said it was a piece of cake!"*

A couple of kids smiled, a few even chuckled—a good start. Feeling encouraged, I kept going with another joke. *"Why was the math book sad?"*. I waited a beat, then delivered the punchline with a big grin. *"Because it had too many problems"*.

This time, more kids laughed, and the room started to feel lighter. Their laughter was shy at first, but as I continued with more jokes, their responses grew louder. *"How do you organize a space party?"* I asked, making a playful face. *"Your planet!"*

By now, the laughter was spreading, and even the quietest kids began to join in. The mood in the classroom was turning; the kids were starting to connect with me and with each other through the silly jokes.

Seeing their smiles, I felt a relief. We were moving past the awkwardness, and I could see the barriers breaking down. *"Alright, one last joke,"* I announced, and they leaned in, eager for more. *"What do you call a dinosaur that is sleeping?"* I paused dramatically. *"A dino-snore!"*

The laughter that followed was full and genuine. The classroom had transformed from a place of caution to one of warmth and engagement. As the giggles subsided, I looked around at their bright faces. *"Thanks for the laughs, everyone. Let's start our day with some fun learning, okay?"*

They nodded, their earlier hesitation replaced by enthusiasm. We had turned a corner together, and as I started the lesson, I knew that we had rebuilt our connection. The classroom was alive with energy, and I felt reassured that we were back on track, ready to learn and enjoy our time together.

The class went well, and as we finished up, one of the kids, curious, looked up at me and asked, *"How do you know so many jokes?"*

I smiled, thinking of my grandfather. *"I learned them from Mr. Perfect, my grandfather,"* I said.

The kid's interest grew, and he quickly asked another question.

"Why do you call him Mr. Perfect?"

Chapter 15:
Why is His Name Mr. Perfect?

A long time ago, there was a man from a small village in the northern part of India. He didn't study much and wasn't interested in school or books. Instead, he spent his days wandering around the village, observing people and learning from their actions.

He was different from everyone else. While others worked hard in the fields or shops, he was often seen sitting under a tree, watching the world go by. He didn't fit in, and people thought he was very imperfect. They couldn't understand why he didn't settle down and do what was expected of him.

This man had a habit that puzzled everyone. Every day, he would collect all the leftover food from the villagers. He would walk far away from the village and throw it away. No one knew why he did this. They thought he was strange and that he had lost his mind.

He was different in many ways. His clothes were often mismatched and wrinkled. He didn't care much about appearances. He used to learn new languages, just for the fun of it. He loved moving around, meeting new people, and hearing their stories. He rarely stayed in one place for long.

While everyone else in the village followed a routine, he did not worry about fitting in. When others his age were busy doing conventional things, he chose a different path. He didn't have a regular job and wasn't concerned about earning money. He was always curious, always exploring.

People called him irresponsible because he gave away what little he had. He didn't save money and often forgot about his own needs. He was seen as someone who didn't have his life together.

There was a time he tried to teach me how to ride a bicycle. He was as clumsy as I was, and we both fell multiple times. He laughed off every fall, saying, "We'll get it right eventually."

His way of living was not understood by many. They saw him as someone who didn't fit in, someone who was always doing things differently. They thought he was imperfect because he didn't follow the norms.

But to me, he was *Madham Mauli*, my grandfather. He was different, and that's what made him special.

When I was six years old, I used to be with my grandfather all the time. His outlook on the world was very different. In every situation, he had a unique perspective. One time, when our neighbor's cow fell sick, he didn't just suggest the usual remedies. Instead, he spent hours talking to the cow, saying that sometimes, even animals needed to feel heard.

One day, I still remember, it was raining heavily. The rain was really loud, and everyone in the village was panicking. They were worried about what would happen. Would there be destruction? I heard my grandfather saying, "How beautiful." He mentioned, "The nature will not harm us; it's our protector. We shouldn't spoil it."

While everyone else was worried the village might flood again, he was just adoring nature. He enjoyed the rain. He went outside the house and stood there, letting the rain soak him. I remember my grandma shouting at him to come inside. He just smiled and said, "If you don't enjoy the rain, it means you're not enjoying life."

After saying that, he pulled me outside too. We danced in the rain, laughing and splashing in the puddles. It felt like all the worries washed away with the rainwater.

Later, he asked me if I felt like eating something. We didn't have any money, but with whatever was there at home, he cooked a meal and told me it was a dish from Tibet. I didn't know if it really was, but it was the best meal I ever had. My grandma kept shouting that he had spoiled the entire kitchen. She blamed him for everything the villagers said about him. She told him how everyone judged him for not having a regular job or a proper lifestyle. Everyone blamed him, including my father.

But he never cared what people said about him. He worked, but he didn't do conventional jobs. One month, he would be a plumber, another month a painter. Suddenly, he would be teaching something to someone. Was he really that imperfect?

Everyone judged him. These thoughts went through my head as we collected the leftover food. I accompanied him, and we fed the dogs that were abandoned on the outskirts of the village.

As we walked back, I couldn't help but ask, *"Grandpa, so all this while, you weren't throwing the food away, but bringing it to them to eat? Why are people so bad, talking about you?"*

He smiled down at me, a kind smile that made me feel safe. *"People don't always understand, Mamali. They judge what they don't know. But you know, you shouldn't always care how much people judge you."*

"But why, Grandpa?"

He paused, choosing his words carefully. *"All it takes is one good gesture, and everything changes. People will start to see the good in you. But don't wait for it. It'll happen when it's meant to. Just live your life on your terms."*

I thought about this for a moment. *"So, you don't mind being imperfect?"*

He laughed softly. *"Yes, I am very imperfect. And that's okay."*

"But Grandpa," I continued, *"everyone talks about you. They say you don't have a regular job, that you're always doing different things. Doesn't that bother you?"*

He shook his head. *"No, Mamali. People will always have something to say. One month I'm a plumber, another month I'm a painter, and sometimes I'm a teacher. What matters is that I am happy and that I am helping others in my own way."*

I looked up at him, trying to understand. *"So, you're not worried about what they think?"*

He stopped walking and knelt down to my level. *"No, I am not worried. I am doing what I believe is right. People will understand eventually. What matters is that you are true to yourself."*

I felt a rush of warmth and admiration. *"You're perfect, Grandpa. You're my Mr. Perfect."*

He squeezed my hand gently, and we continued walking home, the rain now just a soft drizzle. As we walked, I realized that his imperfections were what made him perfect to me. He lived his life with kindness and joy, no matter what others thought.

To me, he was not imperfect. He was just different, and in his difference, I found my own sense of what it meant to be perfect.

Now, back to the present. After sharing these stories, I went on to teach many more classes. I worked hard to help the NGO where I was employed, making it more successful. We helped many children get an education and a better life.

Every evening, I spend time on the terrace with my kids. We talk, laugh, and share stories just like I did with my grandfather. I feel a sense of peace and fulfillment.

Life has come full circle. I am in the place I have always wanted to be. I am happy and content, living my life on my terms, just like my grandfather taught me.

As I sit on the terrace, watching the sunset with my kids, I feel grateful for the lessons my grandfather gave me. His imperfections showed me the beauty of being different and living a life true to oneself.

He was, and always will be, my Mr. Perfect.

A Poem for My Grandfather

Grandpa, you were different,
In a world that didn't see,
Your way of life was special,
And it meant so much to me.

You didn't follow others,
You walked your own path,
With kindness and with laughter,
You always made me laugh.

In the rain, you saw beauty,
When others saw only fear,
You danced with joy and freedom,
You made the world so clear.

You picked up leftover food,
And fed the dogs in need,
You taught me love and giving,
Through every little deed.

They called you imperfect,
But to me, you were the best,
You lived with heart and passion,
And never like the rest.

Grandpa, my Mr. Perfect,
Your lessons guide my way,
In every laugh and sunset,
I feel your love each day.

Chapter 16:
Full Circle

After many days, I am here. Outside the hall, many people are waiting for me to talk. I stand backstage, looking at myself in the mirror.

"Who are you?" I ask my reflection. "Why are you here? Did you make it? Have you achieved what you set out to do? Is this my happily ever after moment?"

I look into my own eyes, searching for answers. I see the little girl who danced in the rain. I see the young woman who worked hard to help the NGO grow. I see the teacher who spends her evenings on the terrace with her kids. All these parts of me are here, together, in this moment.

I take a deep breath and remind myself why I am here. I have a story to tell, a journey to share. I have faced challenges, learned from them, and grown stronger. This is my moment to speak, to inspire, and to reflect on everything that has brought me here.

I smooth down my dress, take another deep breath, and step towards the stage.

"Good evening, everyone," I begin, my voice steady and clear. "I want to start by sharing a little about myself. I was

once a small girl from a small town, but I had big dreams. Dreams so big that even I didn't fully understand them."

I pause,

"In my young age, poverty and shame were our only identity. Every meal was a battle, a struggle to get through the day. Looking back, I realize I was a warrior, facing each challenge head-on."

I glance at the audience, seeing their attentive faces.

"I don't remember a day without troubles. Troubles and obstacles always seemed to find me. But as a warrior, my job was to go through them. And I didn't face them alone. I had people who believed in me, who had immense trust in me. They believed I could become something, that one day, everything would change."

I smile,

"And today, I see my father sitting in the crowd, feeling the proudest he has ever been. My brother, who has and will sacrifice anything and everything for me. Thank you, Gyan. And I can still feel the presence of my mom, who has been my pillar, my mirror."

Now, I have a better house to stay in, good meals on my table, my father is getting healthy, and Gyan is doing his own business. Things have changed.

"Let me tell you all a small story. There was a boy in our village, just like me, who believed education was out of reach. His family struggled every day, and going to school seemed like an impossible dream. But he had a spark in his eyes, a desire to learn and grow."

I take a breath,

"One day, our NGO reached out to him. We provided him with books, a uniform, and the support he needed. At first, he was hesitant. He didn't believe he deserved it. But slowly, he began to see that education was for everyone. He started attending school, studying hard, and soon, his grades improved. He discovered a love for science and dreamed of becoming an engineer."

I look at the audience,

"And today, that boy is sitting right here in the front row. His name is Ravi, and he is a shining example of how education can change a life." Education can change anyone's life. It opens doors, creates opportunities, and builds a future. It doesn't matter where you come from or what your background is. Everyone deserves a chance to learn, to grow, and to achieve their dreams."

I take a moment to look around the room, seeing the hope and inspiration in their faces.

"So, when you see a child with a spark in their eyes, remember that education can make that spark grow. Support them, believe in them, and watch as they transform their lives. Just like Ravi, just like me."

"Every day at our NGO, I see lives changing. Children who once had no hope now have dreams. They are learning, growing, and finding their paths. Mothers who once struggled to provide for their families now have the skills to earn a living. Fathers who felt lost and helpless now stand tall, proud of their children's achievements."

"We are not just providing education; we are providing hope, opportunities, and a better future."

I look back at Ravi, who is smiling, his eyes full of dreams and determination.

"This is why I believe in what we do. This is why I believe in education. It can make all the difference in the world."

"One day, I met Amar, my watchman's son, in the corridors of my college. That moment changed everything for me. He brought a new perspective to my life. I still remember asking him, 'Why aren't you in school at this time?' He looked at me and said, 'That's why I'm in college. What are you doing?'"

I smile at the memory,

"He found me again later and asked if I could teach him and his friends. We started on my terrace. It was a simple beginning, but it meant a lot. It wasn't an easy journey, but it was the start of something important. Teaching them made me realize how much I loved helping others learn."

"Thank you, Amar, for being the spark that lit this fire."

"This journey brought me to the NGO through Jay, who was my college friend. He saw how passionate I was about teaching and helping others. He knew I would be happiest doing this work, and he encouraged me to join."

"Then there is Vaashi Sir, my mentor from college. He has been my pillar, always believing in me and guiding me. Without him, I wouldn't have had the courage to take these steps."

"And this award for being the change in the education world would not have been possible without my grandfather, Mr. Perfect. He meant the world to me. Every time I was down, I found reasons to get back up because of him. He is not here today. I mean, he is on his journey of finding new ways to be happy in life, a wanderer till his last breath. Probably we all should be. We all need to wander for our dreams and go towards them."

"My grandfather taught me that life is about exploring, learning, and never settling for less. He never followed the conventional path, and he showed me that it's okay to be different. It's okay to chase dreams that seem out of reach. His spirit of wandering, of seeking happiness in every moment, is something I carry with me every day. We all should take a lesson from his life and never stop wandering, never stop dreaming, and never stop striving for what makes us truly happy."

Before I end, I want to share one of my hobbies that has been with me all this while. I like writing poems, and I have written one for everyone here today.

Learning is like a fun game,
Where every day, we grow and change,
In each child, a dream can bloom,
In every heart, there's always room.

Life won't always be a breeze,
Sometimes it will bring you to your knees,
But don't let troubles make you quit,
Keep going, and never sit.

Every challenge is a test,
To help you learn and do your best,
With every problem that you beat,
You make your journey feel complete.
Dream big and reach for the sky,
Even when the days go by,
With hard work and a lot of cheer,
You'll find success is always near.
Remember, you can always win,
No matter what trouble you are in,
Keep learning and keep trying,
And you'll be the one who's always flying.

Everyone in the audience starts to clap, and I see people feeling proud of me.

"*I want to thank you all for this award. I do not know if I have changed everything, but I wish to be the change for all. As Vaashi Sir once told me, 'There are a lot of you out there, and you need to be here for them.'*"

"Thank you. I'm Mamali, and this was my story."

About the Book

I was once a small girl from a small town, but I had big dreams. Dreams so big that even I didn't fully understand them. I faced troubles and obstacles every day, but I never gave up. I had people who believed in me, who had immense trust in me. They believed I could become something, that one day, everything would change.

This is my story, a journey of hope, struggle, and finding my way. I don't know if I have changed everything, but I wish to be the change for others. As someone once told me, "There are a lot of you out there, and you need to be here for them."

I'm Mamali, and this is my story. A story of many.

About the Author

Kalyani Mohanty was born on January 2, 1996, in Odisha, India, and has always had a deep passion for storytelling. She recently fulfilled her dream by completing her first book, crafted to inspire young adults through engaging narratives.

Her academic journey began with a diploma from IGIT Sarang, followed by a bachelor's degree from the Government College of Engineering in Keonjhar. Kalyani then earned her master's degree from IIT (Indian School of Mines) in Dhanbad, Jharkhand. She is currently pursuing a doctoral degree in Natural Resources and Environmental Engineering at UPC Barcelona, Spain.

Beyond writing, Kalyani enjoys traveling, cooking, and painting, which showcases her diverse creative interests. Through her literary work and academic pursuits, she hopes to inspire others to follow their dreams.

www.ingramcontent.com/pod-product-compliance
Lightning Source LLC
Chambersburg PA
CBHW020544160726
47991CB00002B/578